"Anything

"Like for you to forgive me for last night?" Mack's voice, deepened by emotion, seemed to slice right through her. Her gaze cut to his and the rough demand in his blue eyes snared her completely. She must have looked confused because he added, "For the stupid things I said?"

"I should apologize, too."

"No, Corrie," he said firmly, taking a step forward. "You had every right to be angry. You've been nothing but wonderful from day one. I'm the one whose been slinging a bushel of mixed signals."

"You were pretty clear last night," she said. Her voice felt rusty, her jaw stiff.

"Yes, if you mean my wanting to kiss you. And liking it. And wanting to do it again."

"You do?"

"God, yes."

Dear Reader,

Our exciting month of May begins with another of bestselling author and reader favorite Fiona Brand's Australian Alpha heroes. In *Gabriel West: Still the One*, we learn that former agent Gabriel West and his ex-wife have spent their years apart wishing they were back together again. And their wish is about to come true, but only because Tyler needs protection from whoever is trying to kill her—and Gabriel is just the man for the job.

Marie Ferrarella's crossline continuity, THE MOM SQUAD, continues, and this month it's Intimate Moments' turn. In *The Baby Mission*, a pregnant special agent and her partner develop an interest in each other that extends beyond police matters. Kylie Brant goes on with THE TREMAINE TRADITION with *Entrapment*, in which wickedly handsome Sam Tremaine needs the heroine to use the less-than-savory parts of her past to help him capture an international criminal. Marilyn Tracy offers another story set on her Rancho Milagro, or Ranch of Miracles, with *At Close Range*, featuring a man scarred—inside and out—and the lovely rancher who can help heal him. And in Vickie Taylor's *The Last Honorable Man*, a mother-to-be seeks protection from the man she'd been taught to view as the enemy—and finds a brand-new life for herself and her child in the process. In addition, Brenda Harlan makes her debut with *McIver's Mission*, in which a beautiful attorney who's spent her life protecting families now finds that *she* is in danger—and the handsome man who's designated himself as her guardian poses the greatest threat of all.

Enjoy! And be sure to come back next month for more of the best romantic reading around, right here in Intimate Moments.

Leslie J. Wainger

Leslie J. Wainger
Executive Senior Editor

Please address questions and book requests to:
Silhouette Reader Service
U.S.: 3010 Walden Ave., P.O. Box 1325, Buffalo, NY 14269
Canadian: P.O. Box 609, Fort Erie, Ont. L2A 5X3

At Close Range
MARILYN TRACY

Published by Silhouette Books

America's Publisher of Contemporary Romance

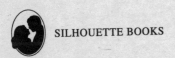 SILHOUETTE BOOKS

ISBN 0-373-27292-8

AT CLOSE RANGE

Copyright © 2003 by Tracy Lecocq

Books by Marilyn Tracy

MARILYN TRACY

Ranging in subject matter from classic women-in-jeopardy scenarios to fallen angels fighting to save the universe, Marilyn's books have placed on several bestseller lists and earned her such awards as *Romantic Times* Career and Lifetime Achievement Awards, and Best of Series. She claims to speak Russian with fair fluency, Hebrew with appalling mistakes and enough Spanish to get her arrested at any border crossing. She lives with her sister in Roswell, New Mexico, where the only aliens they've seen thus far are the critters in their new home, a converted railroad warehouse.

For Dar, who lost Jim but has dear friends.
For Linda, who survived chemo and has dear friends.
And for Mom, who scared us all this year,
but has cool daughters.

Chapter 1

"They say that curses follow blessings," Rita said, snapping a top sheet over the bed. "That's the way it happens. First the good, then the bad."

"Who's saying this?" Corrie asked the housekeeper, not looking up from her notebook. She crossed out a word, penned in another.

"Oh, you know. People. Lots of different people, smart people. Too many good things have happened here, they are saying."

"And there's something wrong with that?"

"There's nothing wrong with good things. Good is good. But when so much good happens…"

"It's time for the bad?"

"Sí, señora, that's how it works." Finished with the sheets and the comforter, Rita plumped the pillows with a vigor belied by her tiny frame. Five feet tall, with black hair and snapping black eyes, she couldn't weigh more than ninety pounds dripping wet and could wrestle the most recalcitrant child into washing behind her ears. "And that Doreen at the post office? She's talking about ghosts again."

Corrie chuckled, thinking of the bold young mother of three who peddled more gossip than stamps. "I should have thought she was too busy with her wedding plans to worry about ghosts out here," Corrie said.

"Oh, Doreen was talking wedding plans long before she snagged that young deputy marshal. See, there's another good thing."

Corrie nodded absently, already back to studying what she'd written. It was less a journal than a song notebook, but as usual, the lyrics were too sharp and pointed, contrived in a harsh fashion. She sighed. She'd come to Rancho Milagro to join her friends and partners, giving up her safe career—or fleeing it—to help run the ranch. But secretly dreaming she could follow her heart's desire, she'd run to the ranch in order to give herself the chance to write songs.

If what she'd penned that morning was any indication of the future, and if Reba McEntire decided to sing songs with a decided bite, Corrie Stratton would be a surefire hit; otherwise, she'd better get back into journalism. No one wanted to listen to songs that dripped with romanticism only to end in a kick-in-the-face at the denouement.

Rita moved to the carpet sweeper and began scratching it across the woven rug. "My mother had a saying, 'Talk about something bad and the Devil won't notice you.' The priest, I don't think he would agree, but me, I think she was right."

"What rhymes with loss?" Corrie muttered.

"You writing a poem? I like the *versos* at church. I know, how about *sauce? Moss?*"

"Or *floss.*" Corrie groaned and closed the notebook for the fiftieth time in a month. She laid her head down on the desk. "Why did I ever think I was a songsmith, anyway?"

"You're writing a song? Like 'Qué Buena Esa Vida'? I like that one. 'How good life is.' Mmm. You write songs like that?"

Corrie raised her head from the desk. "I wish," she said. She pushed up and turned her attention on Rita. "Let me get this right, because so many good things have happened here at the ranch...."

"Sí, like the children coming and being so happy. Like Señora Jeannie falling in love with Chance Salazar and marrying him even if he was a marshal. Like the water coming from the spring after all these years, just like the legend said it would. You coming here, even if your hands still shake and you have no meat on your bones. These things are all good things. Little *milagros.* Miracles. Of course, you know that because you speak such good Spanish." She smiled, then sighed, placing both hands on the handle of the sweeper, looking for all the world like a Henriette Wyeth painting. "Now it's the Devil's turn. Mischief time. Bad luck." She raised her hand in the old sign against the Devil himself, a crooked forefinger over a thumb, making a rough cross.

The doorbell of the hacienda rang, and when Rita didn't make a move, Corrie leaned back, waiting.

Rita looked to the bedroom door and then to Corrie.

Corrie looked from Rita to the bedroom door, sighed and pushed away from the desk.

"Don't go, *señora*," Rita said. "'When the Devil knocks, don't answer the door.' My mama, she says that."

Corrie withheld a shiver and shook her head. It seemed to her that Rita's mother was obsessed with devils and demons. She hoped Rita didn't pass along her mother's little gems to the children. They'd had enough rough times before coming to the ranch that they didn't need a heap of superstitious nonsense clouding their fragile psyches.

The doorbell peeled again, the rich chimes echoing throughout Rancho Milagro's main hacienda before Corrie reached the foyer. If she'd been writing a song about it, the words would have started, *Rita's mama's Devil knocked at the door....*

At least Rita had a mother; Corrie didn't, nor did either of her partners in the Rancho Milagro venture. There seemed some irony in the notion of three orphans tackling an orphans' ranch. There was a feeling of coming full circle and, at the same time, one of embarking into completely new territory. They knew how to *be* orphans, but did they really know how to raise them?

Corrie pulled open one of the heavy wooden doors, sincerely hoping it wasn't another of the tabloid journalists seeking a miracle story.

The man standing on the veranda didn't look like a devil, but how could she be sure these days?

He had his back to her, apparently surveying the ranch outbuildings, a few of the children in the corral and the playground, or perhaps he studied the long view to the Guadalupe Mountains in the distance.

He wasn't dressed in what Corrie thought of as cowboy garb—boots, buckle and snaps—though he still managed to look from the Southwest with his broad shoulders, chinos, crisp cotton shirt and corduroy sport jacket.

If it had been twenty years before, she'd have taken him to be a reporter, but the new breed of journalists didn't wear sport coats or starched shirts, and their pants usually looked several years worse for wear. She ought to know; she'd seen enough of them in her lifetime, and even more than that in the past month.

"Can I help you?" she asked softly.

He turned slowly, as if steeling himself against something unpleasant, and swiveled an unsmiling and scarred face toward her. Though healed, the scars were obvious results of skin grafting, and done by a rather skilled surgeon. The lack of a smile could be attributed to any of a thousand reasons.

Her first thought was that he must have been a remarkably handsome man before whatever accident had befallen him. Rugged, square features, high cheekbones, piercing blue eyes and graying black hair. Then she realized the scars only accentuated his looks, as if he'd been born of tragedy and it and not genetics had carved his fierce features.

He nodded.

She inclined her head in response and waited, her heart pounding a little faster.

"I'm Mack," he said. His voice was pitched low and was somewhat gravelly, as though he spoke infrequently or smoked too much. A blues voice. "Mack Dorsey."

The name seemed familiar, but the man did not. "Corrie Stratton," she said automatically.

It was customary in the Southwest to hold out one's hand immediately upon meeting, greeting or saying farewell. But Corrie wasn't from the Southwest and still found the practice uncomfortable around strangers. Besides which, and to her relief, the screen door still served as a distinct barrier between them.

He gave a half lift of his lips, not, she thought, as if he were trying to smile, but as if trying to remember how. The scars on his face notwithstanding, nothing about him spoke of a damaged man. He looked tough and hard. Cold and unapproachable. His eyes told a story of a sorrow she didn't think she wanted to know. It was too intense, too wrenching. And too challenging. She suppressed the urge to shut the door and suffer the agonies of rudeness rather than continue to stand there facing the imposing man.

"I'm here about the teaching job," he said.

Relieved, she almost smiled. She knew who he was now. Jeannie had told her that a new teacher would be coming by for a personal interview. Jeannie and Leeza had already checked his references and investigated his past. Jeannie just hadn't mentioned that it would be today.

Her partners happened to be in Roswell that day on a shopping run and, perhaps because she'd come to the ranch with trembling hands and jumpy nerves, she hadn't had a hand in hiring any of the crew there thus far. But she'd been there long enough now that Jeannie and Leeza had been teasing her of late that she needed to take a more active role in the ranch governance, not just play with the children. It was all too likely that, in the manner of swimming instructors of old, they'd simply thrown her into the deep end, foolishly confident she would learn to keep her head above water.

This would be her first employment interview, and while she might have grilled heads of state, she didn't have the foggiest notion of how to go about hiring a teacher for the children at Rancho Milagro.

Besides which, the man looked nothing like a teacher. With those forbidding icy-blue eyes, squared shoulders and scarred face, he looked as if he'd be more at home riding in a general's jeep, eyes scanning the horizon for snipers and enemy troops.

"I had an appointment," he said, and held out one of Jeannie's cards with the Rancho Milagro logo emblazoned across it. "At one today."

"Right," she murmured, though she wanted to ask him to come back another day, sometime when Leeza, Jeannie or her husband, Chance, was there to talk with this stranger.

"And it's one now."

"So it is," Corrie agreed, though, typically, she had no idea what time it might be. She was quaking inside. No matter how many interviews she'd done over how many years, and discounting the numerous tough situations she'd found herself in, she nevertheless still suffered from nervous qualms at bridging the first question. The obvious one seemed easier than most. "Won't you come in?"

She pushed the screen door out and waited for him to take it, pulling her hand back before his could come within inches of it.

"Thanks," he said, and let the door fall softly closed behind him as he brushed past her.

She felt the heat he carried on him, and told herself she was imagining things as the day had dawned with frost that covered the ranch. Still, they were in the desert and temperatures could easily soar into the nineties during the daylight hours.

Her hands were shaking as she closed the heavy wood door behind him. Before turning around, she drew a deep breath and whispered the oft-repeated litany that had gotten her through so many bad times in the past and countless interviews after that, *"I'm Corrie Stratton, and if I survived my childhood, I can survive this."*

Mack waited for Corrie to turn around and wondered if she might just stay there, forehead pressed against the wood of the oak door, whispering to herself.

Not that he minded the view, he thought. Corrie Stratton was small in stature with a slender frame. Her curves were imperfectly hidden by her long fall of silky chestnut hair, a baggy but elegant emerald shirt and sweatpants that had seen better days. Her feet were bare and her toenails painted a cheery red that seemed at odds with her lack of makeup and inexplicably trembling hands.

"Corrie Stratton. Aren't you one of the owners of Rancho Milagro?" he asked finally, though the moment she'd spoken to him he'd known exactly who she was. *"And from your National Public Radio network, this is Corrie Stratton. Good night."* Maybe she played a larger role in his reasons for appearing at the ranch in the first place.

He watched as her shoulders straightened and her head lifted before she turned around. Her face was composed now, almost as if she'd never had a stray nerve in her life. He was struck by the change in her. Before, she'd seemed disconcerted, even a little frightened. Now she kept her expression neutral, a small smile playing on her full lips.

She nodded as she walked up to him. She held out her hand, and he had the feeling she'd accomplished the simple act by sheer force of will and, moreover, that she'd rather be on any other planet than standing there about to shake hands with him. And because of that he had no choice but to take that slim hand into his.

As always, the shock of feeling someone else touching the new skin on his hands gave him the sense of déjà vu, as if he simultaneously remembered how he was supposed to feel another's palm and the reality of encountering it through new skin.

He imagined there was something different in Corrie Stratton's fluttering touch. And that something struck him purely viscerally. Whatever the feeling was, it had nothing whatsoever to do with scars, nerve endings or wounds too recently healed.

"I'm sorry," she said.

He released her hand. He wasn't sure what she was sorry about, but hid a smile as she curled her hand into a fist and cradled it against her chest, almost as though she were holding his imprint to her.

Or, perhaps, as if he'd injured her.

"Leeza and Jeannie aren't here today."

He frowned. "My interview is with you, I believe."
She blinked. "It is?"

"That's what I was told," he said. He glanced down
at the business card Jeannie Salazar had given him,
though he knew Corrie Stratton's name was scrawled
on the back with the time of the interview beneath it.
He flipped it over and held it out.

He thought of the endless hours he'd spent listening
to her on the radio and wondering if any woman could
measure up to that incredible voice. She did and then
some. "Yep, here it is."

She glanced at the card but didn't reach for it.
"You'll have to forgive me. I must have forgotten to
jot it down in my book."

She wasn't what he'd expected. He'd heard her
voice a million times, a thousand hours beyond that.
Low and sultry, her subdued voice, with its inherent
sexuality, had led him to picture her to be long-legged,
lush and ultraseductive.

Instead, she appeared scarcely tethered to this
planet, held down by sheer gravity only. The epitome
of petite, she was an almost elfin creature, only some
five foot something, all long, delicate fingers, sloe eyes
and cheery red toenails. And yet, her gaze, somewhat
shy and attempting to hide her nervousness, spoke vol-
umes. And let him know she was lying.

Someone had neglected to tell her about the interview. How he knew this, he wasn't sure, but he knew
it nonetheless. Corrie Stratton wasn't the kind of person who might blame another. He wondered if she'd
have been more nervous or less had she known he was
coming there this afternoon. For the first time in a
long, long time, he found himself curious about a real

someone; he wanted to know what made a renowned radio journalist like Corrie Stratton so skittish.

She pulled her hair up into a rough ponytail that she held with her fist and walked past him to a long credenza-like entry table, rummaged in the upper drawer and retrieved a couple of pens. One she stabbed through her hair—and, amazing him, it held the mass of brown locks—and the other she tucked over an ear. She tugged a notepad free from beneath the hall telephone, flipped over the top few pages, smoothed them down and turned to him, all cool, calm and collected prospective employer.

"If you'll follow me," she said, and led the way across the massive living room through an archway into a dining room that could easily sit twenty people. She took a seat at the head of the table and gestured to a chair flanking hers.

He waited until she sat, then joined her at the table. He took in the children's drawings over a long sideboard flanking the dining table. At least twenty of them had been carefully matted and framed and hung in rows beside a low mirror. The mirror reflected the living room he'd passed through, the fireplace on the wall behind him, some hand-woven baskets, a couple of original Holly Huber oil paintings, and an R. C. Gorman print.

His eyes continued their survey of the room and rested thoughtfully on a simple but highly effective alarm system on the dining room wall. It was the kind that could be triggered by hand, excessive heat or smoke. If he remembered the shriek it produced, it was worse than deafening.

"So," she said, after drawing a deep breath.

"Please tell me a little about yourself." To his delight, she lifted her feet to the seat of the chair and wrapped an arm around her legs. After a glance in his direction, she cleared her throat and lowered her bare feet to the floor, crossing her legs in a decidedly studied, ladylike fashion.

He swallowed the smile threatening to surface. And admired the way she'd pulled herself together for an interview she obviously knew nothing about.

"I've taught for twelve years, have a master's degree in history from Texas Tech and am certified in Texas, New Mexico and Colorado, grades K through 12. And, if you have tennis courts, I can coach tennis, too."

"I see," she said, jotting down something in her notepad. "And what is it that makes you want to work at Rancho Milagro?"

He hesitated and she looked up to meet his eyes. Hers were a deep, rich brown, he saw, like coffee liqueur. Eyes a man could get drunk and drown in. He thought it was a lucky thing she'd made her mark in radio broadcasting; those eyes on television would have made the male population newsaholics.

"I'm sorry," he said. "What did you ask?"

She paraphrased her question about working at the ranch.

He looked away from those liquid brown eyes. "I heard what you were trying to do out here. I liked the sound of it. And wanted to be a part of the miracles." He attempted a chuckle as he finished blurting the raw truth.

He couldn't tell her that he'd wanted to be around the woman who had pulled him through a nightmare of torturous procedures, that he craved a slice of the joy Rancho Milagro apparently served for breakfast. At least he hadn't blurted out that he wanted a new life.

Simply wanted.

He didn't really believe wanting made anything so. He used to, once upon a distant time, but not any longer. He fought the nightmare images that threatened to rise to the surface, the tragic sound of children crying for help, the scent of burning linoleum and, ultimately, the stench of despair. He didn't believe miracles were possible, but he wanted any and all to come his way so much more than he could ever begin to tell her.

He felt dazed as she gave him a swift, conspiratorial smile. A knee tucked back up into her chest. She clasped it and leaned forward. ''Me, too,'' she said.

She, who seemingly had everything, wanted a miracle? What could she possibly want? To meet another king, interview another world leader? What was she even doing on this lonely ranch, miles away from everything?

He didn't voice any of his questions, but apparently his silence seemed to make her potential-employer consciousness take over again. Her leg lowered and crossed again. He resisted the urge to look beneath the table to see if her toes even touched the floor.

She asked, ''What was it that you liked the sound of?''

The miracles—and you, he almost said, lured by her eyes into telling more unvarnished truth. ''The kids. Taking foster kids and orphans, giving them a working ranch and home environment. Letting them have half

a chance before sending them out on their own,"
he said.

He'd wanted, perhaps needed, to come to work
there because the tabloids and news features referred
to the place as a ranch of miracles. When cynical journalists waxed ecstatic, a huge kernel of truth must lie
within the story. And one truth was obvious, the Rancho Milagro partners took in the strays of the world
and offered them new lives.

He asked, "How many do you have now?"

"What? Oh, children, you mean. For a minute, I
thought you meant miracles." She stopped on a rueful
smile, drew a deep breath and continued, "We only
have seven so far. Two are already adopted by Jeannie
and Chance—Dulce and José—but they take lessons
with the others."

"You already have teachers, then?"

"Only one, Melanie Jorgensen, and she's not here
yet. She's arriving in the fall." She released a slight
smile, as if remembering Melanie Jorgensen and liking
the memory. "In the meantime, we've all been pitch-
ing in for various subjects." She made a face as if the
classes weren't going well. "Right now, we're on
home-school status because it's too far to ship the children into Carlsbad schools and because the children
we have now are all somewhat behind in their schooling."

"So this would be a temporary arrangement?"

He realized his question was inept when she gave
him a blank stare. "Temporary? No. Oh, you mean
about the home schooling. Again, no."

He loved the way she couched every answer in formal terms, as if he might misconstrue the slightest

nuance of what she said. It was one of her trademarks on the radio, the bit they advertised before her golden voice came on. *When Corrie Stratton says it's true, it's a fact.*

The woman with the golden voice and truth in her words tilted her head at him. "Eventually we'd like our own status as an official school. But that's a far piece down the road, as they say around here. With the home-school status, however, and with certified teachers, we can still get these kids well grounded in what they need to know to get good college placements."

Her feet crept to the chair seat again. He was sure she was unaware of the fact that one of her arms wrapped around her knees, drawing them to her chest. He was also sure she was utterly unaware how attractive she was.

"That's the object, then?" he asked.

She frowned and looked a question at him.

"What you would want from a teacher?"

"I see," she said as carefully as she had before. "I'm not exactly sure what Leeza or Jeannie would say in answer to that. From my perspective, I think what we want is someone who will be surrogate parent, teacher, friend and mentor with a bit of a kindly uncle thrown in."

"A teacher of many hats," he said, and leaned back in the chair, relaxed for the first time since he'd driven onto the ranch.

She smiled at him—a bit wistfully, he thought. "It's a dream, I know. But..."

"One that's already working." Abruptly, it wasn't just the job he wanted, but to reassure her that the ranch-cum-children's-home dream was already coming true.

"Yes," she said, and gave him the most genuine smile she'd managed with him so far—except when she'd expressed her wish for a miracle.

He felt that smile like a fever coming on, making him feel hot and restless.

"So far it's working." She cleared her throat as if remembering she was conducting an interview. "Are you currently teaching somewhere, Mr. Dorsey?"

"Mack," he said.

"Okay. Sorry. Mack, are you teaching anywhere right now?"

"Nothing to apologize for and, no, at the moment I'm not teaching, so I'd be available immediately," he said.

She gave him a funny look before making another scratch in her notepad. "And when was the last time you were in the classroom, Mr. Dorsey?"

"Mack," he corrected. He realized then that she didn't know who he was, that she didn't realize that he was the so-called hero of the Enchanted Hills incident. *Teacher heroically sacrifices himself to rescue ten students burning in blazing inferno*. And what else was an inferno but blazing and what was a sacrifice when he had lived and five children had died?

For a moment, as so often happened, the cries of the children, both rescued and lost, echoed in his ears and his nose stung from the acrid scent of burning schoolrooms.

Corrie Stratton, the woman with the golden voice and the coffee-liqueur eyes didn't blink. Lady journalist extraordinaire, this tiny scrap of a woman didn't seem to have a clue as to his identity.

He gave a faint and, he hoped, easy smile. "I've been out for two years."

She looked up at him and raised an eyebrow. He must have made some kind of gesture. He found it somewhat ironic that he'd come to Milagro in part to escape the newshounds, the incessant prying into his life, and was now being interviewed by one of the nation's leading investigative journalists and she didn't have a clue about him. Because of that news interest, he had assumed Corrie's partner, Leeza, had known who he was and hadn't asked him to discuss his reasons for being out of the classroom for such a long time when he went through the initial phone interview with Leeza and the secondary meeting with Jeannie. He found himself stymied and irrationally resenting having to reveal the truth about his scars and talk about the many things he couldn't explain away—the pain, the losses. Her gaze traveled from his hands to the scars on his face. "An accident?" she asked.

Could one call a deliberately executed firebomb that killed five children and a cafeteria worker an accident? In a cosmic fashion, perhaps that would be true.

"Yes," he said, and didn't elaborate. He was grateful when she didn't pursue that line of questioning.

She cleared her throat again. "You do realize that you'd have to be living here on Milagro?"

Living on a miracle. Better than the bitter ashes of regret. "That works for me," he said truthfully. He didn't add that it would be an escape. A refuge. Just dodging the media would be a miracle in and of itself.

"And that because we're providing room and

board—and a horse, if you want to ride—we're not offering even close to what could be considered a competitive salary?''

''With the add-ons of the living quarters, food and, of course, a horse, I'm okay with the salary, provided you offer insurance.''

To her credit, she didn't look at his scars this time, though he could see a noticeable rise in her color. ''Of course. That's a given.'' She didn't look up as she added, ''We require a thirty-day probationary period.''

''Accepted.''

Her eyes shot to his. He felt a jolt of something hot and fiery shoot through him. He had to clear his throat before asking, ''Are you offering me the job, Ms. Stratton?'' Her partners, Jeannie and Leeza, had led him to believe this interview was pro forma only.

For all the nights of listening to her voice in the loneliest hours of the dark, believing her stories, fantasizing about her, he suddenly wanted her to ask him to stay, not because he was qualified, but because *she* wanted him to. Knowing a fantasy was impossible didn't make it fade any more swiftly.

''Corrie,'' she said, without answering him.

''What?''

''You can call me Corrie.''

It was like being asked to call Dan Rather, Dan, or Barbara Walters, Babs. But whatever he'd thought before coming out here, despite the needs he'd felt when he saw the opening advertised, he wanted this job now. He wanted it more than anything on the face of the earth. ''Okay. Corrie, then.''

Her eyes met his and he saw the wary denial in her gaze. Disappointment shafted through him. She would say no. She didn't want him as a teacher on this ranch of miracles. Then he saw something else in her gaze. Something confused and alluring, a look that had nothing whatsoever to do with teaching.

He rasped, "Are you offering me the job?"

She shook her head, though her eyes implored him to understand something she didn't voice. He clearly saw her wary rejection. "I...I don't think I can do anything without the approval of my partners, Mr. Dorsey—"

"Just call me Mack." Two could play at that game.

"Mack." He thought she repeated his name as if savoring it. Her eyes flickered and she shook her head. "I don't think I can—"

A horse's angry whinny and a child's scream cut her words off midstream. In the split second of hesitation following the scream, their eyes locked. Hers, he thought, carried a wealth of fear and helplessness, a pleading that he *do* something. His, he was sure, told her he couldn't do a thing to help, that people had died because of him before.

But looking into the depths of her coffee eyes, he felt powerless to resist her. Without a word, he shoved away from the table and was through the doors and across the veranda.

From the time of the scream to his leap from the steps, no more than three seconds could have passed.

A flashy pinto, with a small kid of nine or ten looking like a rag-doll saddle decoration, bucked and lurched toward the hacienda steps, whinnying shrilly and trying his best to rid himself of the child-burr on his back. The boy, all eyes and scrawny legs, screamed bloody murder and held on to the saddle horn for dear life.

Without thinking about it, Mack jumped from the bottom of the steps, directly into the heaving horse's path. The beast shuddered and whinnied anew but skidded to a halt.

Mack heard a swift shriek from behind him. He heard other yells and ignored them. All his attention was focused only on the horse and the small boy perched above him.

The little boy, who had somehow held on during the wild ride, lost his control at the abrupt stop and pitched forward. He somersaulted down the horse's neck to land at Mack's feet.

Mack hooked a leg around the boy and flipped him behind him, not worrying how the boy would fare against the dirt, but terrified that the shivering horse would decide to rear and bring its sharp hooves down onto the child.

Though he knew less than nothing about horses, he instinctively reached for the fallen reins of the horse's bridle and, talking to the horse the whole time, managed to secure them. The horse turned a white, rolled eye in his direction and, trembling, stamped the ground and huffed several times before seeming to realize he was all right.

When he could find his voice, Mack asked gruffly, "Hey, kid, you okay?"

Corrie stood frozen on the veranda steps, both hands holding a scream inside. Fractured images of alternate timelines flashed through her mind, other presents and myriad futures: *Mack Dorsey sitting calmly at the din-*

ing table, handing over references while Juan Carlos flew across the air to thud on the ground with a final groan of pain. Mack and Corrie laughing over something and Juan Carlos trampled by Dancer's hooves. A funeral, a pregnant Jeannie crying in her husband's arms, a headstone with Juan Carlos's birthdate etched and the death date today. Juan Carlos riding Dancer and Mack Dorsey deciding not to come to Rancho Milagro that fine early spring afternoon.

She heard him ask, "Hey, kid, you okay?"

Juan Carlos sat up, perfectly all right, using Mack Dorsey's jeans as a pulley. "Y-yeah, I think. Yeah, I'm okay."

Somehow, Corrie managed to get down the steps despite her watery legs and reached Juan Carlos about the same time the groundskeeper and sometimes groom, Jorge, came limping around the corner of the hacienda, gasping and cursing in little bursts of winded Spanish.

Even as she patted the boy down, trying unsuccessfully to pry him from his grip on Mack Dorsey's legs, Corrie felt like laughing at Jorge's bedraggled curses. Juan Carlos, according to Jorge, would fall down a rabbit hole and be twitched to death by bunny whiskers. Juan Carlos, before the day was over, would have his face torn off by magpies and sewn on backward by prairie dogs. Juan Carlos, if he didn't learn to listen to Jorge, would have to learn the entire alphabet in both Spanish and English backward and forward.

"*Niño,*" Jorge panted, seeing the boy alive and tremulously smiling up at Mack Dorsey, "next time you want to kill old Jorge, just get a gun, okay?" He bent over, a hand on his chest, another on one knee.

"*El hombre* stopped the horse for me," Juan Carlos said, but didn't let go of Mack's jeans. Corrie knew how he felt. Her own legs gave way about then and she sat down in the dirt, one hand on Juan Carlos's shoulder and the other on the toe of Mack Dorsey's tennis shoe.

"His name is Mr. Mack Dorsey," Corrie said faintly. "And you better say a very good thank-you."

Juan Carlos looked up. "Thank you, *señor*. But you made me fall off the horse."

Corrie gave a ragged chuckle that was all too close to a sob. "Not quite good enough, Juan Carlos. Try again."

"Thank you for getting in the way of my horse, Señor Mack."

"J-Juan Carlos!" Jorge sputtered. "You get up right now and say you're sorry." After some effort, the older man stood upright and took the reins from Mack's hands. "I'll take the horse now, *señor*. Thank God you were here."

The two men clasped hands and Mack withstood a hard backslap from Jorge before leaning over to shake Juan Carlos's upstretched hand.

"Take it easy, kid," Mack said.

"You, too, Señor Mack."

Corrie looked up to find Mack's eyes on her, a crooked smile on his lips. He held out a scarred hand.

She put hers in his, felt the smooth skin enveloping hers, let him pull her up, smelled the dust the horse had kicked up, and smelled her own fear and the heady, all-male scent of Mack Dorsey.

She nodded at him. He nodded back.

She smiled and he didn't.

She drew a deep, tremulous breath. "The sooner you can bring your things, the better," she said.

Then he smiled.

Chapter 2

If Mack was surprised that everyone shared evening meals together at Rancho Milagro, the others seemed to find it perfectly normal. Within seconds of his entering the hacienda for a second time that day, he was subjected to a rapid-fire introduction to the rest of the household.

He nodded at the awesomely tall and gorgeous Leeza Nelson, whom he'd spoken to on the phone when he first applied for the job. Leeza was only on the ranch for a short time, Corrie had told him earlier; she had to go back to Washington, D.C., to run her company. He also nodded to Jeannie, another of the partners, and Chance Salazar, her U.S. Marshal husband, and raised a hand to their two kids, Dulce and José. He was reintroduced to Juan Carlos—much improved by soap and water—the ranch hands, Clovis, Jorge and Pablo, and four other children ranging in age from six to eleven whom he didn't have names for yet.

Places were set at the enormous table in the dining room. Only a couple of the chairs were without mats, plates and silverware. Three large pitchers of iced tea with lemons and ice bobbing to the surface served as centerpieces and the cloth napkins adorning each plate all held a different shape.

The housekeeper, Rita—a tiny stick of a woman in her forties—plopped the last dish down on an enormous sideboard before taking a place at the table herself and heaving a huge sigh. "*Señors, señoras,* and *niños*…dinner is ready."

Mack expected the kids to launch from the table and attack the sideboard, but no one moved. Finally, Jeannie held out her hands on either side, clasping her husband's in one and her daughter Dulce's in the other. "Grace," she said. "Juan Carlos? I believe it's your turn."

Mack couldn't remember the last time he'd been a party to saying grace before dinner—some long-ago Thanksgiving when he was just a little squirt, he suspected—and felt awkward taking the little girl's hand seated next to him and Corrie's on the other. Corrie's was dry and warm; the little girl's scrubbed and slightly damp. While Corrie's fingers pulsed and trembled beneath his, the little girl's fingers squeezed his hand, as if offering reassurance, or—in his opinion, far worse—trust.

He bowed his head with the others when Jeannie signaled Juan Carlos to perform the blessing.

The boy cleared his throat and sang out a version of grace he'd obviously been practicing. "Thanks for the tacos, thanks for the beans, and thank you, God, for my blue jeans!''

Mack wasn't the only one who chuckled. And to his combined surprise and relief, no one reprimanded the boy. The little girl, whose hand had rested so trustingly in his, removed it to cover her giggles.

Jeannie's husband, Chance, gave a sharp bark of laughter, followed by deep chortles. Leeza muttered something and, shaking her head, hid a grin that threatened to soften her somewhat forbidding features. Jeannie tsked but smiled fondly at the kid whose gift for rhyme might not meet a holier person's standards.

But Corrie's reaction was the best, he thought. She bit her lower lip while giving the boy a slow, deliberate wink, as if they'd cooked up the crazy blessing together. And when the boy gave her a cocky thumbs-up, Mack realized that they had. No wonder miracles happened around this place.

When she glanced at him, and recognized by his answering look that he'd caught her coaching, she flushed a little, shrugged, and by tilting her head at Juan Carlos, let him understand that she didn't want him to say anything. Mack remembered her conspiratorial smile earlier that afternoon. Before the bucking horse episode, prior to her offering him the job, when she'd asked him why he wanted to be at Rancho Milagro, and, at his answer of wanting to be a part of the miracles, she had hunched forward, guileless, conspiratorial, and said *''Me, too.''*

The little girl next to him leaned against him, still giggling, sharing her laughter in her shaking shoulders. He resisted the urge to place his arm around her. Corrie's wish of teacher-cum-kindly-uncle might be her dream, but in the real world of lawsuits and traumas, a simple touch could so easily be misconstrued. Still, the little girl pressed against his arm and rested her forehead on his forearm. He couldn't help but chuckle at her helpless laughter. And for a fleeting moment, wondered how long it had been since he'd laughed.

"Okay, tonight, even though we have a newcomer, kids get to go first," Jeannie said. "And Juan Carlos? Keep your fingers away from the alarm."

Seven chairs, including the one next to his, scraped across broad, burnt-sienna-colored Saltillo tile and seven giggling children raced to the sideboard.

"Chance? Would you pour the wine? Thanks, honey. So, Mack, what do you think so far?" Jeannie asked him over the children's clamor and clanking of serving utensils.

Mack accepted the glass of wine from an openly smiling Chance, and nodded at the kids. "I'm intrigued," he said.

"Good," Jeannie said, and put her hand over her own empty wineglass and grinned up at her husband. "Can't, remember?"

Chance kissed her and lowered a hand to caress her neck. "Worth it?" he asked.

"Every minute," she said, taking his hand to kiss it.

Mack felt riveted by the overt love in their eyes. He'd read one of the tabloid accounts of the undercover marshal and the ranch owner falling in love, the first of the long string of Milagro's so-called miracles.

"Jeannie's pregnant and not letting a single second of the pampering get away," Leeza explained in a dry voice. He'd have suspected a snipe hiding in her words if he hadn't seen her eyes, which were, he thought, starkly and unknowingly wistful.

Mack resisted the urge to look over his shoulder for a disaster lurking in the shadows of the large dining room. Kids laughing and jostling in line, adults relaxed and easy, mixed cultures and backgrounds, beautiful scents rising from the food spread on a lavish sideboard; it all seemed too good to be true.

Instead, he nodded, as if Leeza had asked him a question. He gave a rusty smile at the glowing-faced and obviously happy Jeannie. She smiled back at him and raised a protective hand to her scarcely showing belly. "I'm sure it all seems pretty strange to you right now," she said.

He hoped the kids returning to the table, scraping chairs and trading friendly insults in a mixture of Spanish and English, precluded the need for an answer from him, for if he'd had to give one, it would have been in the negative. It didn't seem strange; it seemed completely alien. It was too perfect. And anything too wonderful, too perfect was sure to have a downside.

"Señor Mack?" Pablo rose and waved his hand at the sideboard. "You first, yes?"

Mack was in awe at the array of foods prepared for the Rancho Milagro crowd. Far from mere tacos and beans, the fare included an enormous roast beef tenderloin, a salad with seemingly every known vegetable and some cheeses he didn't recognize, home-baked bread with sun-dried tomatoes, a large bowl of herb-and-butter pasta, and a host of soft or crispy finger foods that would normally be served as hors d'oeuvres.

As he helped himself to a healthy portion of the

dishes, knowing from the quantity that he needn't stint whatsoever, he listened to the easy conversation behind him.

"What's this, Corrie?" one of the kids asked.

"Fried grasshopper," she answered promptly. "With enough tempura batter, it tastes just like lobster."

"Eew!" chirped one of the boys. "Not really?"

After the pause that followed her question, several of the kids laughed, and so did the little boy. "It doesn't taste like a grasshopper. It tastes *good!*"

"See?" Corrie said, her sultry voice all the more alluring when filled with teasing laughter. "It's all in the batter."

"And this?" another kid piped up. "What's this?"

"That's the snake that was bothering me by the back gate. Deep-fried rattlesnacks, I call 'em."

Beside him Pablo chuckled. "That Corrie, she's like a kid herself."

Mack turned his head to look at her.

No employer facade masked her face now. Pablo was right; she almost looked a child herself as she pressed against the table, her eyes sparkling, her face flushed, and a soft, inviting smile curving her generous lips. "And those little ones that look like fried spiders? Well, there you go. I decided we needed to wage war. So instead of nuking the little critters, we're frying them."

"Yuck," one of the boys said.

"That's what they're called. Yuckums."

Juan Carlos laughed and popped one of the spidery confections in his mouth. "Mmm," he said after crunching noisily, swallowing elaborately. "They're *delicioso*."

Mack found himself mesmerized by Corrie's face. She looked so at home, laughing with the children, not an aunt or a mother, a mere child herself, lost in the teasing moment, full of merry delight and wonder. So different from the woman who had greeted him at the door, the one who had been unable to remain standing as she ran to the little boy thrust behind his legs, and certainly not the famous newswoman the world knew so well. Here, she was one of the kids, her sultry, well-known PBS voice a beacon and her smile a lighthouse of warmth.

Something inside him twisted and pulled. If he'd met her only a few years before, he thought he'd probably have moved heaven and earth itself to spend some time with her.

Mack's dinner partner, the little girl with the hapless giggles and the trusting grip, studied Juan Carlos's antics with now-solemn eyes. "It's squash," she announced to the table at large. "I helped. It's just squash from the pantry place, not spiders. We graded it. It gets an A-plus. Corrie wouldn't make us eat spiders."

"*Señor?*" Pablo asked.

Mack realized he'd been staring at Corrie, holding up the line for dinner. He jerked his attention back to the sideboard, muttered a quick apology and took one of the rattlesnacks and a couple of the yuckums to add to his plate before moving back to his chair.

When he sat down, the little girl with the big black eyes and missing teeth scooted a bit closer and whispered loudly, "They really are squashes. Don't worry.

It's nothing scary.'' She patted his hand and, in doing so, ripped something loose in his long-closed heart.

Corrie, who had almost convinced herself that it was just another rollicking evening at Rancho Milagro, had nevertheless been all too aware of every single move that Mack Dorsey made. She'd heard his throaty chuckle at Juan Carlos's cheeky prayer, witnessed his surprise when no one took exception to it and saw the precise moment little Analissa had gotten under his skin forever.

She'd felt him jolt when Analissa patted the scars on his long, beautiful hands and told him not to worry; the squash confections weren't scary. Everything in him seemed to stiffen, as if electrified. And she'd heard him take a hitching breath, as if what he was about to say he swallowed instead.

The children fell as silent as only kids could be while eating with total concentration. The adults talked about various ranch details, feeding the cattle, the shopping trip that day, adding a new corral for the horses in the spring, speculation on adding an official schoolhouse. It should have been just another normal evening, everything casual, simple, but it seemed thrown into chaos with the addition of Mack Dorsey, who contributed nothing to the adult conversation and seemed ill at ease with the children's chomping noises.

Pushing her own plate aside, Corrie glanced at Jeannie, so at home in her special element of creating a home for disparate souls, and saw her friend's gaze resting on Mack. To Corrie's certain knowledge, Jeannie had never judged anyone, and Mack Dorsey appeared no different. Jeannie's eyes conveyed nothing but warmth, welcome and a sincere level of curiosity.

Next to her, however, Leeza stared at Mack as if he'd suddenly sprouted horns. Her eyes widened and a look of recognition flooded her face. She straightened and stretched out her hand to Jeannie, who, although not breaking her easy smile, looped slender fingers over her friend's wrist.

Leeza ignored the message. "Mack, I'm sorry, aren't you—"

"Leeza," Jeannie murmured in warning. Corrie tensed, waiting for Leeza to continue. Much as she, herself, might want to know about Mack, she didn't want to put him on the spot.

"I finished my plate, *señoras*. Can I have dessert now?" Juan Carlos interrupted.

"Let's see that plate," Jeannie said, and with no more than a cursory glance, gave her opinion that dessert was in order. "But only after everyone helps clear these dishes."

Seven bodies bobbed up from the table and Leeza's question faltered in the wake of so much clatter of dishes and silverware.

Corrie hid a smile as little Analissa snatched Mack's plate away mid-bite with a blithe "You're done, right Señor Mack?" and a happy grin when he nodded, before she added confidentially, "I'll be right back. You stay here, 'kay?"

"Okay," he said, wiping his mouth on one of the cotton napkins and nodding at the intent young face waiting for an answer from him.

"Right here," Analissa commanded.

"Just for you, I'll wait right in this very spot. Can I move while you're gone?" A half smile played around his lips and Corrie could tell Analissa had melted the frost in his eyes.

The little girl nodded solemnly. "But you can't go away."

"I won't," he said.

"Promise?"

Corrie frowned when he hesitated. What possible harm could it do to promise the little girl he'd be there when she got back? It would only take a matter of minutes while the kids deposited the dishes and brought in Rita's amazing anise-flavored *biscochitos* and homemade ice cream.

"Promise?" Analissa demanded. "You have to promise. And cross your heart."

"If you hurry back, I'll be here," he said, and reached his hand out as if he would stroke the little girl's hair. His hand hung there for a moment, then dropped back to his lap as if the child's aura had burned him.

Corrie's breath tangled in her throat, both at the look of withdrawal in Mack's gaze and at the lack of promise to the little girl. He'd agreed, but it had been a half promise at best, not the whole she'd asked for. Luckily, Analissa didn't notice. She only beamed brightly, her partially toothy grin brightening the dining room as it always did. Before the child reached the door to the kitchen, she managed to lose most of the silverware on the two plates she smashed together, and chip at least one of those plates against the door-jamb.

Leeza leaned forward again, having retrieved the errant silverware and handing them to Jeannie's adopted daughter, who was indulgently smiling at Analissa. "Mack, aren't you the one who—"

Chance's wineglass toppled into Leeza's lap and he swore as he stood up, napkin in hand, and mopped up the wine. He apologized to the table at large for being every kind of a clumsy fool, then before a shocked Leeza could even remonstrate, he leaned down to say something in her ear before turning to kiss his wife soundly.

To Corrie's surprise, Leeza flushed and shot Mack an apologetic look.

Corrie knew Chance wasn't clumsy; his every move was measured and slow, calm and deliberate. The marshal had spilled his wine on purpose, stopping Leeza's questioning of Mack.

Why? What didn't he want brought out at the Rancho Milagro dinner table? What did he know about Mack? How he acquired his terrible scars, what accident befell him?

Why was Chance avoiding her eyes? Why did Mack appear so tense and stiff beside her? And why did her journalistic instincts rise so readily to the surface when she wasn't working in the field anymore and never, ever wanted to again?

"Mack," Jeannie asked, commanding attention as she stretched and leaned back into her chair, "what period of history interests you the most?"

"Prehistoric," he said swiftly.

"Why is that?"

"Because the lines were so clear in those days. Survival was all that mattered. Find a cave, find a mate, make a home, go out and hunt a bear or two for food, clothing and fat for the fire. Simple. Hard, but simple.''

''Sounds rather macho,'' Leeza murmured.

Mack waved a hand in a noncommittal gesture but nodded as he took a sip of wine. ''Oh, there were plenty of matriarchal tribes then, too, but the bottom line was still the same. Survival.''

''What about happiness?'' Corrie asked, twisting her own untouched wineglass around, wondering why his answer might mean something important.

''Happiness?'' he asked.

Corrie thought he repeated the word as if he'd never heard it before, didn't know its meaning.

He turned to look at her, as if he were trying to imprint some unspoken knowledge on her, and answered, ''Happiness was a matter of security, safety, ensuring everyone in the cave had shelter, food and water. Safety. That's all that matters.''

She heard his switch from past to present tense. ''But—''

The door to the kitchen burst open and a beaming Analissa sailed through, carrying a tray laden with ice cream in paper cups.

''Dessert,'' she called, and, taking small, heel-to-toe steps, made her careful progress to Mack.

He looked at her as if surprised she'd returned, as if the little girl, all by herself, was a miracle on this ranch in the middle of nowhere.

He gave one of those half lifts of his lips. The little girl nodded solemnly. ''You're here,'' she said. The smile that followed her words could have lit the entire city of Carlsbad.

Mack cleared his throat. ''I'm here.''

Little Analissa turned her beaming face to Corrie. "Just like he promised."

From her place beside Mack, Corrie saw a muscle twitch in his jaw, not as if he were laughing, but as if he were biting back some emotion too bitter to swallow. "Just like," she said.

"And you're gonna stay here with us, right?" Analissa asked, leaning forward, tipping the tray dangerously.

Mack caught the tray before the ice cream in the Dixie cups slid to the floor. "I'm here," he agreed.

Analissa launched herself at him, her baby arms thin and spindly against his broad, rock-hard shoulder. The tray teetered dangerously, but not half as much as Corrie suspected Mack's emotions might be tipping. "To stay?"

Corrie rescued him. "To stay, sweetie. He's here to stay," she said, reaching out to stroke Analissa's silky hair.

Mack didn't say anything. He set the tray on the table and gently dislodged Analissa from his arm as he pushed to his feet.

The rest of the children poured through the open doorway, treats in store, and raced around the table, making sure everyone had at least two of the prized *biscochitos*.

"You're not leaving, Señor Mack?" Juan Carlos asked.

"Really, you must try one of Rita's *biscochitos*. She makes the best anywhere on earth," Leeza said.

"He's got to go," Analissa said, all six of her years showing, and twenty-five more to boot. "But he's staying here now. Corrie says. He's going to stay with us.''

A cheer went around the table, with a few I-told-you-so's from Juan Carlos and nods from Jorge.

Corrie thought Mack's face would have paled had his scarred skin allowed it to do so. Instead, he only stood above them all, seemingly carved in granite, and as acutely uncomfortable as a man could possibly be.

''I'll walk you out,'' she said.

''It's not necessary,'' he answered. ''Thank you all for the wonderful dinner.''

''Food will be here tomorrow morning and again at lunchtime and then again at supper,'' Jeannie said. ''It's the Rancho Milagro way.''

''And we'll talk about classes in the morning,'' Leeza said.

''And I'll show you my new saddle for Dancer,'' Juan Carlos said. ''I can ride again next week. I'm grounded now.'' He made a face that was more grin than grimace. ''Because I rode Dancer without permission.''

''And I'll draw you a picture,'' Analissa said, curling her hand into his pant leg and dragging on it. ''It will have you in it, and Corrie, and Dancer the horse, and Jeannie, and Chance, and Dulce, and—'' she looked around the table, her dark eyes questing ''—and Clovis, and Pablo, and Rita and everybody.''

''Thanks,'' Mack said, but Corrie thought he looked as if the whole lot of them had stretched a hot bed of coals for him to walk across. He turned to the living room as if made of wood—stiff and resistant. If she hadn't witnessed for herself his reactions to each of the children, she might have wondered how he might

act as a teacher. But she'd seen his smile at Juan Carlos's joking prayer and his tumbling for Analissa.

"Sleep tight," Jeannie called gently.

Corrie saw Mack hesitate in his walk. He raised a
hand as if in farewell.

Juan Carlos called out, "Be careful, Señor Mack.
And watch out for La Dolorosa."

Mack stopped and half turned back to the group at
the table.

"What, you afraid of ghosts, Juan Carlos?" Dulce
sneered.

"No way! But Rita said people in Carlsbad have
seen her lately. And Jorge said—"

"That's enough, Juan Carlos," Jeannie interrupted
gently but firmly. "Those are only stories. There are
no such things as ghosts." She looked at Analissa with
meaning in her gaze.

"But—"

"No buts. Good night, Mack. I'm glad you're join-
ing us."

Mack raised his hand again, not in a wave, but more
in a gesture of frustration. He nodded and made for
the front door.

"See you tomorrow, Señor Mack," Analissa called
out.

The door slammed behind him before the little girl
could hear an answer.

"He'll be here," Jeannie assured her, drawing the
child to her lap. She ran her hand over the little girl's
hair.

"I think he wants us," Analissa said, pressing her
face into Jeannie's chest. "I think he needs to be
here."

Corrie thought so, too.

Chapter 3

Mack was grateful for the icy chill of the night. He gulped at the air like a drowning man. He could hear the laughter filtering through the French windows of the veranda and could still feel the impression Analissa's little hand left behind. He listened as the heavy door opened and closed. And knew without looking around that it was Corrie Stratton who'd followed him outside.

She was the last person on earth he wanted to see at that moment. She made him want to tell her things, hard things, raw things he'd rather keep locked inside.

"It takes some getting used to," Corrie's sultry voice said from behind him.

He thought about all the times he'd listened to her voice pouring out of the radio into the dark hospital burn unit during his long recuperation. She'd been a friend telling a late-night bedtime story, a woman who talked with kings and soldiers far away and relayed their stories back to those waiting to hear her voice again.

"Overwhelmed?" she asked, stepping up to join him at the railing surrounding the broad veranda.

For some reason, he didn't want to lie to her, and he wanted to hear that beautiful voice, so he didn't answer her directly. "How long have the children been here?"

"Let's see. José and Dulce were the first and they came the same week about a year ago. I think Jason came next, then Tony, Jenny and Juan Carlos. Then Analissa. She's been here about three weeks. She's a doll."

"Tell me about them," he said.

Corrie leaned against the railing. "No one knows where José came from. He just showed up here one day when Jeannie was first finishing renovations on the place. We've searched and searched, but no luck, and if José knows, he's not saying. Jeannie and Chance have moved five or six mountains to try to unravel the paperwork involved in adopting a child who has seemingly sprung from nowhere. They're not through the wringer yet, but with the status here for long-term foster care, we all hold high hopes. Dulce was orphaned as a child and was shuffled from one foster home to another until she was so filled with attitude and distrust that she could hardly say her name without spitting at you."

Mack wondered if Corrie knew her cadence had slipped into a storyteller's rhythm, graceful and filled with hints of magic. He leaned against one of the large, round viga-pole supports and said, "She'll be a beauty, that one."

Corrie agreed and continued, "Tony has parents, but his father is in prison and his mother placed him in the foster-care system because she couldn't handle things. He's been in the system now for three years."

"A lifetime to a kid his age."

"One third of it, anyway. And Jenny's father took off shortly after she was born and her mother's in the hospital having her fifth child. Five children, five different fathers. Not one of them involved with their contributions to the world."

"What about her brothers and sisters?"

"The grandmother can manage them, she says, but claims Jenny wouldn't do anything she was told." A sharp note edged Corrie's normally soft tones.

"That's the little girl who never said a word tonight, right?"

"That's our Jenny. She's eleven and behind three grade levels, though there's nothing wrong with her mind."

"And Juan Carlos?"

Corrie gave a soft chuckle. "That child is a handful. He came to us from a group home in Portales. That's a town about a hundred and thirty miles north and east of here."

Mack knew where it was. He'd finished his student teaching there on an exchange with Texas Tech. "What brought him to you?"

"Firecrackers in the toilets," she said matter-of-factly, with a strange little smile. "I guess the system figured that we were so remote, we probably didn't have plumbing, so he couldn't hurt anything."

"And has he?"

She looked up at him and smiled. Again, he felt that fever. "He hasn't blown anything up, if that's what you're asking. Has he gotten in trouble? That's his middle name."

"And what about the other boy, the one with the crush on Dulce?"

"Jason? Does he have one?" Corrie asked. "I should have guessed. He's always really quiet around her. He's here for just a few weeks. His mother took off when he was three. His dad's a fireman and was called up to go to one of the fires in the Northwest."

"No relatives?"

"Not a one. Poor guy."

Mack didn't know if she meant the father or the son. "And Analissa?"

"She's our resident ray of sunshine. Her parents skipped out on her years ago and her aunt's just gone into drug rehab for the umpteenth time. The authorities found Analissa when they busted the aunt for dealing. The poor baby was literally wearing her own waste and so hungry she couldn't keep anything down for the first three days."

"Jeez," Mack said. "Did they bring her straight to you?"

"After the hospital, yes. You can see why she wants promises."

"Everyone wants promises," Mack said roughly.

"Do you?" she asked.

Her question jackknifed through him. He felt the heat of the fire that changed his life. He heard the screams of children calling for help. He smelled the putrid-sweet scent of burning flesh.

"No," he said too harshly, then realized his quick exclamation sounded like a denial.

"And why is that?" she asked almost lazily. Dreamily.

"Are you doing a story?"

"No. Are you ducking the question?"

He couldn't help but chuckle. He could see why she'd managed to interview the amazing personalities she had over the years. "No. Yes. I don't know. I just don't believe in promises anymore."

"Miracles, but not promises?"

"If you like," he said.

"That's rather sad, Mack Dorsey."

"Realistic."

"Is there a difference?" she asked, and pushed herself away from the railing. "It's been my experience that reality and sorrow seem to travel hand in hand."

"That's life," he said, still refusing to look directly into her eyes.

"Has it always been like that for you or did something happen that made you feel that way about life?"

He didn't dare answer her, although just being with her almost made him want to.

"Not everything is sad," she said quietly.

"But some things are too sad to bear." He thought of the parents waiting outside the schoolhouse that day, the way they held on to each other, as if the weight of their tragedy was pulling them down to the ground.

"That's what Jeannie used to believe, after her first husband and baby died. We thought for a while we were going to lose her, too. When she cried, it came from her very soul, not just her heart."

"I didn't know," he said. He felt as if he were choking.

"Then she moved here and found her miracle."

"Chance?"

"And Dulce and José. This place. All of the children."

"And you?" he asked. "Have you found your miracle?"

She turned away from him a bit. "It's a miracle enough just being here," she said in a muffled tone, and he knew she was avoiding his question. She had a look of such longing on her face he wanted to put his arms around her and tell her that she deserved more than just being here, that a miracle was waiting for her just around the corner. But she, who had been trained to listen for the truth, would hear the lack of faith in his voice. He kept silent, watching her tuck her hands into her loose sleeves and hunch forward, giving herself the hug he hadn't dared give her.

"It's cold out here," she said.

In other circumstances, he'd have agreed, but with her standing too near him, it felt anything but cold.

"Last year at this time, it was nearly a hundred degrees in the shade."

He made some noise he hoped she'd take for assent, though he wouldn't have known about the weather; he'd still been locked up in a hospital at this time the year before.

"What made you go into teaching?" she asked.

He grimaced. "It sure wasn't the opportunity to mold young minds."

"No?"

"I was one of those problem kids, you know the

type, the cutup, the class clown, the kid who would never sit still or shut up.''

The look she gave him let him know how remotely he resembled that person now. He was surprised to find that notion troubled him. Until the incident that changed so many lives, including his own, he'd been secretly proud of the fact that one principal hid in his office to avoid his protests over how some of the children were treated. Stuffy teachers wrote copious memos about Mack's out-of-the-box disciplinary tactics. Mack had been vaguely pleased to be called a rebel, proving the old adage that some kids never grow up.

But, despite her overt disbelief in his ever having been anything resembling a class clown, she understood where he was going with his story. ''So you chose to change the system from within?''

''Something like that. I was a seventies kid, so the schools were stuffed full of half-baked ideas from the sixties, trendy notions from the seventies and economically based concepts predicted for the eighties.''

She smiled. ''I was there. I know what you mean. Happy faces and dollar signs.''

He nodded with a half smile. ''That's it. The kids become guinea pigs for the latest educational theory. And when the program doesn't work, it's dropped—thank God—but the kids still lose. Big business was helping pick up the tab, so bottom lines became the focus—''

''—and the bottom line in school terms is standardized tests.''

''You've got it.''

''And you wanted to change this?''

"Let's say, modify it. I'm a firm believer in the individual."

"Why not go into administration?"

He gave a mock shudder. "I'm inherently anti-paperwork."

"And rebels with a cause don't rise to the top in administrations."

He found himself liking her, despite his desire to steer clear of personal involvements. He'd admired her from the privacy of his hospital room, listening only to her voice. He'd liked her clarity, her compassion and her attention to detail. Now, standing beside her on Rancho Milagro's broad veranda, he found himself warming to her in a way he'd thought lost to him forever.

"I imagine you were a rebel, also," he said.

She gave an abrupt gurgle of rueful laughter and shook her head swiftly. "Anything but," she said. "I was the good little girl who always did precisely what she was told."

He had trouble accepting that notion. She'd traveled the world, been in some of the most dangerous places, come back with heart-wrenching stories of pain and hope. A good little girl would avoid such situations like the plague. "How about later?" he asked.

"Exactly the same—always a follower, never a leader. A true coward, in essence."

He shook his head, not necessarily disagreeing with her but unable to reconcile his preconceptions of her with what she stated was the reality. The Public Broadcasting System's motto for her ran through his mind. *"When Corrie Stratton says it's true, it's a fact."*

"I'd better get going," he said. Once upon a time, he'd have lingered on this veranda, clung to the time with a pretty woman and a chilly night. Back in that time, he'd have believed in futures, been blind to the pitfalls and dangers that lurked in the shadows.

"Oh. Okay." She looked understandably confused.

"Good night," he said gruffly. He curled his hand into a fist to avoid raising it to her silken face.

"Do you want a flashlight to get back to the bunkhouse?" She turned to face him. The movement was abrupt and unexpected.

He wished she hadn't turned to face him. Her eyes were too luminous in the light cast from the windows, her face too guileless and, for some reason, wistful. He could read the curiosity there and a tinge of sorrow or pity. But he couldn't see the quest for the news story he'd half accused her of pursuing only moments before. He saw a lovely woman on a cold, moonless night, a woman who had come to offer comfort or perhaps mere camaraderie, and he'd closed her out.

It was best that way, he thought. As he'd told her, he didn't believe in promises. Lost in his thoughts, he'd forgotten her offer of a flashlight.

"No, thanks," he said, "I can see my way. You'd better get in before you freeze." But he was the one who turned to go.

"As Juan Carlos would say, watch out for ghosts," she said.

"I'm used to them," he said.

"Plural?"

She was too quick, could hear too much. He turned back to face her but didn't quite meet her eyes. "Plural."

"As in, you're used to more than one ghost."

"As in," he agreed, almost enjoying the interplay.

"Are you speaking metaphorically or literally?"

"Both," he said.

"A man who speaks on multiple levels. Hmm. And talks in riddles."

"We all have ghosts," he said.

"But most people call them baggage, not ghosts."

"I could say I'm not most people."

She gave a slow smile. "I think I'd agree."

He tried a smile in return, but it felt odd on his lips. "I think I'll turn in," he said, lying through his teeth. If tonight were like any other, he wouldn't sleep until nearly dawn.

"Good night, then," she said. "Dream of the angels."

One angel in particular, he thought. "Right," he said. "You, too."

"Always," she said, rocking against the cold. She didn't seem like a child then; she was everything a man could possibly want on a lonely night. And if he didn't walk away from her that very minute, he'd find out exactly what kind of a miracle it would feel like to have her in his arms.

He gave her a stiff half wave and got off the veranda as quickly as he possibly could. He wasn't far enough away, however, not to hear her clear voice murmur, "What are you hiding, Mack Dorsey?"

Chapter 4

From her suite in the main hacienda, Corrie could see the light on in the teacher's bunkhouse and knew Mack Dorsey was awake as well. He'd looked tired, even exhausted when he'd hurried from the veranda, but somehow she wasn't surprised to see his silhouette pacing behind the curtains in the wee hours of the morning.

She was sorry he was out there alone. After a terrible incident the year before when a truly evil man kidnapped Dulce and José in an attempt to force Jeannie to turn the ranch over to him, Jeannie and Chance had decided the ranch hands' sleeping quarters should be much closer to the main hacienda and a new wing had been added. The former staff bunkhouse had been converted to a large, communal-style teachers' living quarters. But Mack was the only one there now.

Part of her wanted to go offer him some comfort,

see if he was in pain, or simply see if he needed some little item he might have forgotten. The other part, the rational side, told her that whatever made him restless was none of her business and she'd be well advised to let him alone.

She turned back to her notebook. *He walks alone, late at night. Ghosts trail behind him, calling his name.*

She groaned—the same could be said of her. Too many ghosts, too many harsh words, too many people claiming her past.

She tossed her pen aside before turning off her own light, as if shutting him out—both physically and mentally.

The narrow aperture of her curtains let Mack Dorsey's lit window shine like a full moon with tidal-wave intent. His shadowy form became a sharp focal point. She held her breath, watching him walk back and forth across the curtained lens.

Feeling like a voyeur, Corrie yanked her curtains closed and turned over on her bed so she wouldn't be able to even imagine she could see his pacing figure. After a few minutes, she swore and sat up in bed. She dragged open the curtains, her eyes automatically seeking the false moon of Mack's window. Though his silhouette was no longer visible, the light remained on.

Corrie checked the clock on the nightstand. Half past three in the morning.

She sat for several minutes, waiting for the light across the drive to turn off, and when it didn't, she sighed and swung her legs out of bed. She dragged on the pair of sweatpants she'd worn earlier that day and shoved her bare feet into a pair of boots Dulce had given her, not caring that they were two sizes too big.

She snatched up a bottle of aspirin from her bathroom cabinet, a book from the bulging bookcase on the wall and, not questioning why, a pen and empty notebook from atop her desk. She shoved all these items into the pockets of the elegant duster Leeza gave her two months ago and opened the exterior door to the veranda.

She shuffled across the broad expanse of driveway to the guest quarters and hunched in her duster as if snow lay on the ground, shivering in the cold desert air.

She marched up the stairs of the teachers' quarters, but, as she raised her fist to the front door, her need to help Mack Dorsey dissolved and so did her resolve. She back stepped, feeling like a fool, hoping he hadn't heard her determined scuffles across his narrow porch.

He was a grown man, for heaven's sake; not one of the wounded children that needed tending as if he were a little bird with a broken wing. His cold eyes could lance evil at eighty yards; he wouldn't need a painkiller for the bruises inflicted by some drunken uncle or father. He wouldn't need a book—and a soft voice—to lull him to sleep, or a pen to write his experiences down. He would know how to survive until morning.

One of the porch steps creaked beneath her too-large boots as she turned to go. As if the stray sounds were an alarm system, the bunkhouse door flew open and made an enormous clang as the heavy metal hinges collided with the brackets against the side of the house. Light spilled from the teachers' quarters, incandescence escaping into the night.

Mack Dorsey stood silhouetted in the light, naked to the waist, barefoot, and standing as if he anticipated a grizzly to rush him. His knees were bent, his bare feet spread apart, as if he anticipated a need to move quickly. He held his hands out from his sides as though she might attack him.

"It's me," she said. And when his eyes strafed the brightly lit driveway at the main house and jerked back to where she stood, she realized how foolish she sounded. "Corrie. Corrie Stratton."

He muttered a curse before slowly straightening.

"Sorry," she said. "I didn't mean to—I was just…"

"It's okay," he growled. The light behind him blocked her from reading his face.

"New place," he said gruffly

That he was in a new place didn't account for the hours of pacing. "I saw your light on. I thought perhaps you needed something?"

He turned his head toward the main house, eyes zeroing in on the only light visible, then, back to her. "You were up at this hour?"

"Drink of water," she lied.

"Me, too," he lied right back at her.

"Oh. Of course. So you don't need anything?" At best her question sounded lame, at worst it sounded like a come-on. She blushed.

Luckily, he didn't seem to read meaning into her words. "You and your partners have thought of everything. Except for clothes, I wouldn't have had to bring a thing."

And he wasn't wearing many of those, she thought. "Jeannie gets all the credit," she said, and hoped he didn't hear the breathlessness in her voice.

"She deserves it," he said.

She shivered against the cold. Despite his lack of clothing, he seemed impervious to the deep chill and she wondered if his many wounds, the scars she could only faintly discern in the dimness, blocked the sensation of cold.

"Well...thanks for thinking of me," he said. His hand ran the length of his torso, a wholly unconscious gesture, but one that robbed her mouth of moisture.

"What?" she asked.

"Thanks for thinking of me." There was a bitter note in his voice.

She'd thought of little else since she opened the front doors to find him standing there for an interview. But at his words, she felt like a three-year-old being dismissed by a social worker.

"Okay. Sure. As long as everything's okay," she said, her voice faltering. "I'll—I'll just go back now." She turned, embarrassed she'd come out there, disturbed at the fact that she had, and that she'd done so armed with a handful of items more suited to welcoming an adolescent than an adult who had obviously survived more than his share of hardship. And then to stare at him like a love-starved teenager. She might be love-starved, but she wasn't a kid anymore.

However much she might be acting like one.

I'm Corrie Stratton, and if I survived my childhood, I can survive this.

Mack felt like a heel. All she'd done was come to check on him. She'd seen his light on at three-thirty in the morning his first night on the ranch, and had come out into the cold out of simple kindness and concern for him. And he'd greeted her as if she were a terrorist, was curt to the point of rudeness, then capped it off by lying to her and making her feel like she'd intruded.

"Wait. Please…?"

She stopped but didn't turn around. "Yes?" Given her voice, even that single questioning syllable sounded like a chord straight from paradise.

"Do you have any aspirin?"

She slowly revolved back to face him and dug into her pocket. She withdrew a paperback, a notebook, a pen and, finally, a bottle of aspirin. She handed him the plastic bottle.

"Thanks," he said, working at the childproof cap. He had to fight himself not to ask about the other items she started to shove back into seemingly rapacious pockets. But he knew instinctively that she'd brought them for him for some reason.

"Here, let me," she said, bridging the gap between them as she stuffed the last of her things back into her pocket. She held out her hand for the bottle and he gave it up without a struggle, careful not to touch her. He was too aware of her standing so close to him in the night, too aware of his own near nudity, his terrible scars she didn't so much as look at, and the way the merest hint of a breeze on the cold night air seemed to tease his newly formed skin.

She flipped the aspirin bottle open and held it out at an angle, apparently prepared to shake them into his hand. Her hands trembled so much that only three astrin fell onto his hand and a few more disappeared into the ground. He closed his palm around her shaking fingers.

"Did I scare you when I threw the door open?"

"Yes…and no," she said, with simple honesty and not a single hint of accusation.

He couldn't resist lifting his free hand to cover the tiny one he had trapped. "I'm sorry," he said.

She gave a half grimace. "Nothing to be sorry about," she said. "It's no big deal."

He felt her hand fluttering in his, a small wild bird. He lifted his fingers and hers took wing. As she'd done when he'd arrived at the ranch, she curled her hand in to her chest.

"Thanks," he said, though he wasn't sure what he was thanking her for.

"You're welcome," she said, but that liquid silk voice of hers seemed to be thanking him instead.

For a moment, an invitation to come inside his new home curled around his tongue. But it tasted too perfect, too sweet. And he was no longer a man who believed that good things were possible. They were only to be desired. But just for a moment he wondered if her skin would feel as smooth as her voice, if her hair would smell as sweet as the expression on her face.

"I hope the aspirin helps," she said, and with a little wave, she turned away from him again, but this time without the look of hurt rejection or the blaze of painful color staining her cheeks.

He let her go, but stood outside until she was back at the main house and inside. He waited until he saw

her light go out, and continued to wait until all h
could see was his own breath freezing in the air.

He dry-swallowed the aspirin left in his palm an
went inside the bunkhouse. His new skin tingled, bo
from the cold and from thinking about Corrie. H
thought about how her hand had felt in his when h
shook it earlier in the day, and how it shook in hi
during the dinnertime prayer. How it quivered beneat
his fingers just now.

What would make a woman of the world, an ico
like Corrie Stratton, so nervous that she trembled? .
possible answer popped into his head, only to be r
jected. A woman with Corrie Stratton's backgroun
her voice, her looks, wouldn't be rendered vulnerabl
around any man, let alone a teacher with more sca
than God should allow.

What kept her awake at night, watching him pac
the floor some two hundred yards away? What we
her ghosts? What was the miracle she sought?

Strangely, once back inside, he felt sleepy. H
wasn't exhausted, restless or even weary. He was ju
sleepy. More strangely still, he fell asleep almost im
mediately after turning off his light.

But not so strangely, he dreamed of a woman wit
delicate fingers and an angel's voice, and somehov
in the dream, he knew she carried miracles in her co
pocket and, in the wake of her magic, he started t
believe the promises in her eyes.

Chapter 5

Mack avoided Corrie like the proverbial plague for the next few days, which, given the size of Rancho Milagro, should have been easy. And could have been if it weren't for the infernal family meals.

During his convalescence, Mack had lain in a darkened room, listening to the radio, and had fantasized about the woman behind the lovely voice. On the ranch, over family-style meals, seeing her laughing with the children, giggling until tears ran, or solemnly taking in a child's tale of the day's activities, made him acutely uncomfortable, as if he'd rummaged through her dresser drawers without her knowledge.

The woman who'd interviewed heads of state and painted word pictures of the global political climate on the radio, sat barefoot at the dinner table, one arm around a child, the other holding her raised knees, as if needing to be grounded. With every gesture, she revealed her heart, her longing and her love for her two partners and the hodgepodge collection of children.

And he wanted her. Fiercely, with a sharp hunger that surprised him in its simplicity and raw desire. And because he wanted her, he told himself he needed to stay as far away from her as humanly possible. He'd come to Rancho Milagro looking for peace, seeking a place where he could make a difference, not expecting any more than that.

On his third night at the ranch, little Analissa was regaling them all with a story of Leeza attempting to ride the gentle old mare, Plugster. "And then she screamed like this—ooh!—and her face turned all red like the flowers in the living room and her eyes got really big, like this...."

Mack half listened to the story but really was watching Corrie. She, in her usual bent-knee perch, sat with her head tilted to one side, her long chestnut hair spilling loose from its twisted ponytail and falling across one shoulder. A tender smile played on her lips. Her eyes were dreamy and soft, alight more with love for the child than humor over the story the little girl told.

Mack found himself holding his breath. What would it feel like to have that look turned on him? As if reading his thoughts, she shifted her gaze to his. For a single second that seemed to last an eternity or two, her expression didn't change. Then her eyes focused on his, and her smile faltered.

They might have been alone in the room, the little girl's story mere background music. Something seemed to leap between them, an electrical arc, a seemingly invisible ribbon of connection. He had to close his eyes to shut her out. No wonder she had been able to pry secrets out of the most hardened political figure. One plunge into the warmth of her rich dark eyes, and a man wanted to reveal every secret he had locked up inside him. At least, this man ached to do just that.

When he opened them, she'd looked away, but wasn't watching little Analissa anymore. She was staring at the wall above the sideboard, her eyes unfocused, not looking at the children's drawings framed there. Color bloomed in her cheeks and her arms were wrapped around her knees. Her long fingers plucked at the loose folds of her trousers and trembled noticeably.

As was becoming his habit, he left the rollicking dinner table earlier than the other adults, needing to get away from all their noisy camaraderie, but most of all to hide from Corrie's too-discerning gaze. He had lesson plans to organize, schedules to prepare. He could do laundry, smear vitamin E oil on his many scars in a vain attempt to make them slowly fade. He could walk the fences, check the locks and pace the back corral.

He could do anything rather than sit next to this beautiful woman who made his body come alive and his heart thunder in his chest.

He'd come to Rancho Milagro looking for a miracle, certainly, but nothing remotely as miraculous as Corrie Stratton.

Before the fire, before the scars, he'd had a vague dream of a happy home. Something unformed, yet present, a wife, children, even barbecues on lazy Saturday afternoons with neighbors and relatives bringing potluck dishes.

But he'd given up on that sort of dream in the aftermath of a shattered afternoon two years before. He'd come to Rancho Milagro for a chance to teach again, to stop the screams of dying children he couldn't save. He had to cling to that knowledge. Even if Corrie Stratton made him want other things, like dreams lost to him now and definitely better left that way, he had to stay focused on his new life. If he let himself, even for a moment, relax his guard, begin to feel safe again, he might falter when needed most, and, as he knew all too well, people could die as a result.

Even though Rancho Milagro sported a staff of ranch hands, a groundskeeper, a federal marshal and several women and children, Mack had taken to walking the perimeter of the hacienda grounds each night after dinner. Both the solitude and the careful survey served to bring the nights into focus.

For all their concern over the children at Milagro, even the marshal seemed too casual with their safety in Mack's opinion. A madman could hide in the shadows of the great adobe barn and capture the stray child sneaking out to feed a carrot to one of the horses. A carelessly tossed cigarette from one of the ranch hands could ignite the bales of hay and the whole place would become an inferno. An unlocked gate could allow danger to waltz through.

Luckily, as the children were society's lost, there weren't many undesirables who would come after them, though he understood that the infamous El Patron, a man with too much money and delusions of power, had done exactly that only a year before when he took José and Dulce from the ranch. As evil as that man was, what was to stop him from exacting revenge from prison?

Vigilance could avoid many a disaster. Sometime in the last two years, that had become Mack's talisman-like phrase. He might not feel comfortable with relaxed dinner conversation, and may have a case of the might-have-beens for Corrie Stratton, but he was right at home letting his eyes comb the shadows, his hands check the fences, and his ears strain for a misplaced footfall.

Corrie hid the disappointment she felt as Mack left the table early for the third night in a row. She'd caught the look of longing on his face as he listened to the children swapping the day's adventures and the unreadable look he'd turned on her. The first she wholly understood. As one raised without a family, she regarded mealtimes at Rancho Milagro as among the most precious of all moments. But she didn't understand his reserve around them all, herself in particular. It was as if she'd personally done something to make him feel unwelcome.

She felt herself flush when she turned back from watching his evening departure to find Jeannie looking at her with speculation. "We're too rowdy for him," her friend said.

"We're too rowdy for anyone but some old rodeo hands and three crazy women from back east," her friend's husband, Chance, said. He dropped a hand over his wife's.

Pablo leaned forward and lowered his voice. "I'll tell you this much, the man's a natural teacher. I never saw Juan Carlos pay so much attention to anything anybody has to say. Ten minutes more this morning and the boy would have believed Mack if he'd told him the moon was made of goat cheese.''

Clovis, one of the ranch hands, agreed with Pablo's assessment and added, "I'll tell you something else, the man's obviously been through the wringer, like with all those burn scars, but he's strong. He was showing some of the kids how to do calisthenics and resistance stuff—what do they call that? He used a word—''

"Anaerobics," Leeza supplied.

"That's it. Anyway, the guy's as solid as a rock. And he had all the kids jumping up and down and in pretty good rhythm, too. And doing judo stuff.''

Corrie remembered the stance he'd taken when she'd disturbed him a few nights before. All muscles, wary fight-ready position, and skin impervious to the night air. He'd suffered skin grafts for burns?

"I like him," Rita said. "He brought all the children to the kitchen yesterday. He had them all making dog biscuits for the puppies.''

"Dog biscuits?" Leeza asked, laughing. "We hire a teacher and get a doggie chef?''

"*Sí, señora,*" Rita said. "And making the children double the recipe by using mathematics. And then half the recipe. And they had to measure everything out using the cups and spoons. Then they had to sell them to one another. The big cookies were two dollars, the medium ones only one, and the tiny ones—''

"I made the little ones," Analissa called out from the next room, leaving no doubt of a child's capacity for eavesdropping.

"*Sí,* you did," Rita agreed mildly. "The little ones were fifty *centavos.* And he made them do all the adding and subtracting themselves. I never had a teacher who used real life as lessons."

"Good idea," Leeza said, flushing a little. As the financial wizard of the partnership, Leeza had struggled with the mathematics lessons for the children, and, thus far, to zero avail. Tony had complained he couldn't even see the little boxes she wanted them to write in, and Juan Carlos had done his crossword-puzzle style. Analissa drew in Leeza's account books. Jenny had just cried.

"What do you think of him, Corrie?" Jeannie asked.

Corrie hoped no one could see the blush that seemed to stay in her cheeks these days. "I think he'll work out fine," she said. She felt as if she was betraying him somehow by talking about him behind his back. She almost had to laugh at the notion. She'd made a career out of talking about others, sharing others' thoughts, dreams and foibles, and publicly at that. Why would talking about one Mack Dorsey make her feel uncomfortable?

"Well, I like him," Chance said, pushing to his feet. "And so does José. And that kid can read people better than any shrink."

They all chuckled and, following Chance's example, started clearing the table. After leaving the kitchen, Corrie stopped Leeza. "Remember the first night Mack was here? You looked as if you recognized him, or remembered something about him. What was it?"

Leeza gave her a blank stare anyone on earth but

Corrie and Jeannie would have taken for complete un-
awareness. However, Corrie had known Leeza since
college. The three orphans had forged a sisterhood that
transcended blood.

"Tell me," Corrie said.

"I don't have a clue what you're talking about,"
Leeza said. She gave an exaggerated yawn and looked
at her wristwatch. "It's late and I've a couple of calls
left to make or the known financial world will collapse
in its tracks."

"Leeza—"

Corrie was surprised when Leeza cupped her face
in her cool hands; the woman seldom showed any sign
of affection. "Rest easy, newshound, the man's been
checked out and then some. Chance just stopped me
from being a dimwit about Mack's burns. Good
night." And she dropped a kiss on Corrie's forehead
and sauntered away toward her office.

Corrie raised a hand to her forehead, as if Leeza's
offhand good-night kiss were imprinted there. It might
as well be. She'd known the woman fifteen years and
had never once felt its like. They'd hugged upon rare
occasion; they'd linked arms at Jeannie's first family's
funeral. They'd cried on each other's shoulder from
rare time to time. But never a kiss.

It was the simple kiss that let Corrie know her friend
knew something about Mack Dorsey. She could easily
drive into town and hop on the Internet and search for
herself, and if that proved fruitless, she had countless
sources from which to draw to find out everything
about Mack Dorsey's life. But facts and data weren't
what made her slip on her duster to head outside to

look for him. She wanted to know what he was feeling.

She knew, if no one else had noticed, that every night Mack had been there, he hadn't gone directly to the teachers' quarters after leaving dinner.

She'd watched him through the French doors or from her bedroom. Each night, he walked to the front gates and checked the locks. He melted into the shadows out by the barn. Sometimes she'd seen him strolling along the fences beyond the corral, his hands running the straight lines of wire, testing the barbs occasionally, or pulling at a strand to make sure it was taut. Another time she'd glimpsed a shadow out beside the well house and suspected he was inspecting the locks on that door as well.

His weren't the casual perambulations of a man working off a heavy meal, nor did he seem particularly fond of stargazing. The nightly roaming had all the earmarks of a man afraid of something. Or acting as guardian.

The teachers' quarters were still dark, so she made for the barn. She didn't see him in the broad, open area, nor could she find him within the stalls. The tack room was empty of all but the smell of leather and molasses oats. The riding ring, a recent addition to Milagro, stretched behind the barn, flanking the empty cattle pens. Mack wasn't there, either.

As she turned to go back through the barn, someone grabbed her and roughly dragged her outside into the lambent moonlight.

She barely issued a squeak of surprise and, when she saw who had hold of her, offered no resistance as he propelled her away from the barn and into the soft

starlight. She stood quiescent in his grasp, searching
his shadowed face. Only her rapid heartbeat betrayed
her reaction to him, and that he couldn't have per-
ceived.

She didn't know why she'd followed him outside,
nor could she begin to explain, even to herself, why
she'd felt no shock when he'd manhandled her to the
riding ring behind the barn. But when he growled a
curse before lowering his lips to hers, she found she'd
sought him in the dark for precisely that reason.

He tasted of the honey he'd poured on the *sopaipilla*
he'd had for dessert and she fancied she could draw
it from his tongue like nectar. His lips were both gentle
and rough, more as if he warred with himself than with
her. His breathing was steady at first, then ragged as
he pulled her even closer.

When he slid a cold hand onto the curve of her
neck, she couldn't withhold a moan. Her knees threatened to buckle in a purely primal reaction. She clung
to his coat as if to a life preserver, feeling she was
going down.

Instead of withdrawing, he plundered, his tongue
thrusting into her, demanding, taking. One of his
hands tangled in her hair, spilling it free of her loose
twist, while the other ran surely down her arm only to
plunge into the warmth beneath her duster. His hand
against her thin blouse felt as cold as ice, and made
her gasp as it slid around her back to pull her even
closer to him.

As though the forceful side of him had won whatever battle he'd waged earlier, he ground her against
him, letting her know with absolute certainty how
strongly she affected him.

Corrie's experience with men had been limited to a few relationships with colleagues in the news business, men who lived for the next story, the next big assignment, and the camera lens or the microphone. As they did in work, they only skimmed the surface of relationships. Their approach to life was that too much information killed a good story; skill, charm and knowing when to wrap things up were all that really mattered. They applied the same reasoning to personal relationships.

Mack's passion was the complete antithesis of casual. His breathing was ragged, his body tense and hard. His hands shook with the need that raged through him. And it sparked something in Corrie that she'd never encountered before, an ache that came from her very soul.

A little voice deep inside her seemed to cry out in relief—*"Ah, at last"*—and with such desire and sincerity she literally throbbed from it.

He could have lowered her to the ground beneath them and she wouldn't have raised a protest. He could have led her to his room and she would have gone willingly.

Instead, he yanked his head back, as if snapping awake. He held on to her shoulders, keeping her at arm's length, confusing her, making her want to push back into him.

"You scared me," he said.

If she were Leeza, she might make some quip, like "boo," and step right back into his embrace. If she were Jeannie, she might try verbally analyzing the reason she'd scared him and why that fear translated into a kiss of such passion that she was still gasping for breath.

As it was, she was only Corrie and didn't know how to ask for more. She never had. So she stood there, an earthquake survivor in the midst of violent aftershocks.

Mack waited for Corrie to say something, anything that would douse the fire that raged inside him. Instead, she gazed at him with unblinking dark eyes, unreadable in their vulnerability. She could have been outraged, though God knew she'd responded. She could have been hurt, though he could see no pain in her eyes. She might even have laughed it off, but he could detect no sign of humor.

She looked like a doe caught in the headlights of a speeding car, neither fearful nor alarmed, but rather simply and acutely *aware* of a certain something about to happen.

He couldn't, in all honesty, apologize. He didn't feel the least sorry for the kiss. In some wholly id-driven portion of his mind, he realized he'd been waiting for this hero's reward for two long years. Through the long, lonely nights of recovery, listening to her voice over the radio, she'd spoken to the best part of him. That the worst part had wanted to drag her to the ground and tear her clothing free of her glorious body couldn't pull the apology from a mouth that still could taste her.

He slowly drew her to him again. She came without the slightest resistance. Her body molded to his. Her hands slid around his waist and held him close. Her breath played on his collarbone.

"Ah," she said, as if finding something she'd lost sometime.

"It's late," he said raggedly, pulling back from her.

"Yes," she agreed, letting him go, with her hands if not her eyes.

"I'll walk you back to the house."

"I'm fine."

"I'm not leaving you out here."

Something flickered in her gaze and her lips parted slightly, as if she were reviewing things to say, comebacks that might leave him lying on his face in the middle of a child's riding ring. But all she said was "Halfway, then."

He reached for her arm to take her elbow, but she stepped forward first, dodging him. He moved back to have her walk through the barn door ahead of him. Her hair, silky soft folds of it, spilled down the back of her duster, as dark as the coat itself, and he caught the light, lemony scent of it. His hands tingled in memory of how tresses of it had fallen across his fingers, ribbons of satin he'd bunched in his fist.

"What are you looking for at night?" she asked.

"Excuse me?"

"When you come out and walk along the fences, what are you looking for?"

He couldn't see her face in the darkness of the barn, but he suspected she would be wearing her radio-interviewer face. "Just walking off dinner," he said.

"Checking the main gate locks? Making sure the well-house door is barred?"

He hadn't realized he'd been so obvious or that anyone had noticed. Even though she couldn't see him, he shrugged. "I don't want the kids getting into mischief."

"Ah. That makes sense," she said, but her tone let him know she didn't believe that to be the only reason he patrolled at night.

They cleared the barn. The main house seemed ablaze in lights across the broad dirt drive. One of the four lab-cross pups barked once and subsided immediately as if recognizing them in the dark.

"It's amazing to think that only a year ago there was nothing here but a few broken-down buildings and some owls and field mice," Corrie said, looking at the ranch house. "Now it's more home than anywhere I've ever lived."

Mack thought her statement sad but didn't say so.

She turned to him and held out a hand. She waited until he took it in his. "Halfway," she said.

"Corrie…"

Her eyes, which had been leveled somewhere around his chin, lifted swiftly to his. "That's the first time you've used my name since that first afternoon you came here. Why do you have such a hard time saying it?" she asked. "You use everyone else's on a daily basis. But not mine. Why is that?"

He could hear no accusation in her tone, only a puzzled question. He thought of her deer-in-the-headlights awareness and answered truthfully, "Because I don't want to kiss *them*."

Her eyes widened and for the first time that night he caught a hint of total surprise, as if he'd said the last thing on earth she'd expected.

"Good night, Corrie," he said.

"Okay," she answered abstractedly.

He turned away from her and started toward his quarters. A few paces from his front steps, he looked back at her. She was still standing where he'd left her, her gaze locked on her outstretched hands, her forehead furrowed in a considering frown, her lips parted and smiling faintly.

Chapter 6

Corrie tried revising some of her lyrics until the early hours of the morning, but the light in the bunkhouse held more allure than the awkward rhymes and rough rhythms. She didn't don her coat and fill her pockets a second time. She merely watched the muscled silhouette walk the floor, remembered the feel of his lips on hers, and sadly wondered what kept him from his bed, driving him from sleep.

And wondered if he knew that when he'd kissed her, he'd driven all hope of sleep from her.

Corrie studied him the next morning and again later that afternoon and could see no signs of insomnia on his chiseled features. His eyes were shadowed but not by lack of sleep, just by whatever demons haunted him. Unlike her, his hands were steady and sure and his gait even and deliberate.

"Pablo was right about him." Jeannie came to the corral fence and leaned against it beside Corrie.

"Right about what?"

"The kids. The way they take to Mack. Look at them. They're like filings to a magnet, a few at a time, until suddenly they're all there, leaning and tugging on him."

"Yet he holds them at arm's length."

"Do you think so?"

"Look at him. It's as if he's somewhere else. His thoughts, anyway."

"They don't seem to mind," Jeannie said.

"They trust him," Corrie said slowly, and with no small amount of admiration. It was rare that a group of orphaned or abandoned children would so readily take to a stranger, especially one who was their teacher.

"So do I," Jeannie said.

"Why?"

"Why don't you?"

"I didn't say I didn't. I just want to know what it is about him that makes you trust him. What do you know about him?"

"Aside from excellent credentials and references, he's a natural with the kids. A pure natural. And I like the way he takes his job so seriously. He hasn't even asked whether or not he has weekends off, did you know that?"

Corrie grinned. There were no days off at Rancho Milagro. Jeannie claimed there were no days off from family. There were getaway times, vacations, excursions, but no one punched a clock or logged overtime.

"I keep getting the feeling I should know about him," Corrie said.

"Like what?"

"Like—something. I don't know."

"Well, Ms. Prizewinning Journalist, you could always do some research on him. Or maybe you don't want to know too much and just don't want to admit it," Jeannie said.

"And this bit of oracle-esque speech means what?"

"Ah…the oracle knows all, reveals but a crack in the large picture frame of life."

"Gag."

Jeannie laughed and relented. "I think you're curious about Mack because he appeals to you. And you don't want to play Corrie the journalist, but Corrie the woman."

Corrie couldn't mask the blush, but said, "You can be inexpressibly corny sometimes, Jeannie."

"And you can be blind as the proverbial bat. When was the last time you indulged in a little romance?"

Corrie thought of Mack's intense kisses the night before. A little romance didn't feel possible with him. If she indulged, as Jeannie called it, she would be engulfed, swamped, enveloped. There would be nothing lighthearted about it.

She watched the children gathered around Mack. Almost exactly as Jeannie had described, first two had come, then a third, until within the time it took to tell about it, all the Milagro kids were there, leaning on him, tugging at his sleeves or his jeans, all talking at once, except Jenny, who seldom spoke.

Mack seemed almost oblivious to the noise, the jostling, even the attention. He merely kept walking toward the barn, four or five children hanging from his arms and legs, as if he did this every day and had done so for centuries.

"Do you suppose he was an orphan, too?" Corrie asked.

"Why would you think it?" Jeannie asked back.

"I don't know. The way he keeps his emotions in check, maybe. The way he doesn't share much of himself." She thought of his saying he'd been the class clown, how serious he was now. She remembered the internal war over kissing her, the few things he'd said afterward.

"He's got kids hanging all over him," Jeannie pointed out.

"Yes, but it's more like he's allowing them to be close to him physically, but he's not hugging or holding on to them."

Corrie thought about her own background. Raised without brothers and sisters, spending years in an orphanage and a series of foster homes, striving to stay in the background, not make waves, she'd chosen a sideline lifestyle, hiding behind a notepad and a microphone. She'd kept her world colored with facts and data, not personal opinions. She'd completed assignments, never initiated them.

She understood the children, because she connected with them on a child's level, knew their fears of rejection, their terror of the unknown. But she didn't believe Mack went into teaching for the same reasons. Teaching wasn't a solitary profession.

"Give him a chance," Jeannie said softly.

Corrie turned surprised eyes in her direction. "I didn't mean I wanted him to go—"

Jeannie flashed a grin. "I didn't think you did. I just don't want you to worry about him too much."

"Deal," Corrie said.

"Speaking of deals...I came out here because we've just had a call from the Eddy County Human Resources Office and they have a little boy who needs to be picked up this evening. They're still searching for his mother so they want us to wait until after dinner. Poor baby was abandoned at the office itself. His name is Pedro. He's a youngling, just a smidge older than Analissa. That'll be good for her, she won't be the only tiny tot.''

"Someone abandoned him at the office?"

"That's about the size of it. It's food-stamp day and the place was packed. When everyone cleared out, there was one little boy left. They've called everywhere they can think of. We're the last resort, I'm told.'' She gave a half moue. "At least there's an option for these kids now.''

"Do you want me to go pick him up?"

"Would you, honey? Leeza's packing to go back to D.C. tomorrow.''

"What? So soon? I thought she'd be out here at least another month or two before leaving again.''

"She's calling it the last merger—she says it like 'The Last Supper.''' Jeannie chuckled then sobered abruptly as she said softly, "And we're going back, too, remember?''

Corrie had forgotten. She supposed she'd wanted to forget. Jeannie's first family, her husband and baby daughter, had been killed by a drunk driver three years before and the anniversary was upon them. She wanted to take her new family to the graves in D.C. and have the families meet in a rather unique nostalgic and welcoming ceremony.

Before Corrie could comment on the ramifications

of that trip, Jeannie continued briskly, "Chance has patrol tonight and I'm supposed to be getting ready for our trip. Pablo has some hot date. Jorge can't drive for a week until his new glasses are ready and Clovis—"

Corrie chuckled. "It's okay. I don't mind."

"But I don't want you driving alone at night with a new little one. Can you take Mack with you?"

Corrie thought of his hands roaming her body, the fire in his kisses. "I'll be fine by myself," Corrie said quickly.

"Please? I'd feel so much better. That's a long way to walk if the Bronco breaks down or something. And it'll be cold."

Corrie put up her hands to forestall further exhortations. "Fine. If he's game, so am I." She'd never been able to resist anything Jeannie wanted. It was part of the reason she'd agreed to be a partner in what Leeza had called No Rancho Yetto.

Less than an hour later, the minute dinner was over, she and Mack were seated side by side in the front seat of the ranch's Bronco, the children gaily waving them off.

The silence in the car was worse than heavy; it seemed a physical presence was sitting fatly between them, blocking any attempt at casual conversation.

Mack's arm rested on the seat back, his fingers nearly touching her shoulder. She could have sworn she felt his proximity and her body tingled in anticipation of his touch. His scent seemed to take over the interior of the Bronco, a rich, sunshine smell mingled with a faint exotic spice.

If he moved at all, the sound of his jeans rasping

against the seat commanded her full attention and she had to fight not to look his way, to keep her eyes from dropping to those same jeans. When he leaned forward to adjust the vent, she stilled, imagining him leaning into her to place his warm lips against the soft curve of her neck.

When he cleared his throat, she almost groaned aloud.

She couldn't seem to think of a single thing to say that wouldn't reveal how dramatically he affected her. All her journalistic training deserted her, letting her know full well she'd done the right thing by abandoning that career—she only had skill, had never done it by instinct. It had been daily torture to question others.

Here in the darkened car with Mack, she felt too confined, too restless. Why couldn't she be like Leeza and just coolly announce she wanted to have an affair with him, state the time limits and be done with it? She had to choke back a bitter laugh. If she did such a thing, she would literally die of embarrassment. It simply wasn't in her nature to state her own needs, her own wants, no matter how much every particle of her seemed tuned to Mack Dorsey. Besides which, she wasn't sure she had it in her to enjoy a casual affair. And there was nothing casual about Mack. Nor the confusing way she felt about him.

If he didn't say something soon, she thought she would likely start screaming.

Mack felt the thirty-mile ride to Carlsbad lasted at least a decade. Every time Corrie moved her hand from the steering wheel to her lap or to adjust the radio, he had to steel himself against the feel of her touch. He berated himself for wishing she would brush those slender, trembling fingers across his arm or his leg and put him out of his misery.

He ached to say something to her, anything that would break the tension that saturated the cab of the Bronco. At the same time, he was afraid to open his mouth for fear he would blurt out every nuance of his past, of the tragedy that ripped apart his life and any hope of a future.

Even if he managed to keep the past buried, he still had a thousand things he wanted to tell her. Something about her compelled a man to talk. He wanted to tell her that he admired the way she truly listened to the children and didn't talk down to them. He could reveal that he'd listened to almost every report she'd ever made from inside or outside the United States. Or that he liked the way she giggled like a little girl herself. Or that she tasted like honey and wine and smelled of lemons and that he hadn't thought of anything else since he'd held her in his arms.

But he said nothing and blamed the kiss the night before for the silence that pummeled them, for the very air between them that seemed filled with static, crackling with his past, his lost hopes, and all the wild fantasies he harbored about her.

He only had to move his hand a few inches and he would be able to stroke her satin skin. He didn't have to move at all to take in her delicate scent.

At the junction for the highway, she changed gears and her knuckles grazed his thigh. He jumped as if she'd burned him and she shied away as painfully. Had he been able to chuckle about it, the moment might have passed without notice. As it was, the silence between them seemed to gain even greater dimension.

The sheer proximity of sitting so close to her drove him crazy and her skittishness only made it worse. It made him too conscious that she was all woman, all alone, and most of all, alone with him.

When she finally pulled up to the Eddy County Human Resources Office, the notion of escaping the Bronco filled him with abject relief. He reached for the door and was already out of the car when he realized Corrie wasn't moving. He turned to look a question in her direction and found her as he did the first time inside Rancho Milagro headquarters, her head averted, her eyes closed, and whispering to herself. At the end of her little prayer or whatever it was, she drew a deep breath, held it, then let it out in a rush.

"What do you whisper to yourself?" he asked, speaking for the first time since they'd left the ranch. His voice, damaged by the disaster two years before, seemed raspier than usual.

She turned to him as if surprised he stood in the door of the cab. Even in the waning evening light, he could see the blush rising to her cheeks. "I—nothing important."

He knew she was lying. Whatever she whispered, it was vital, but something she didn't want to reveal. Strangely, considering how desperately he wanted to avoid delving into another's life, he found himself hungry to know more about her. Everything about her.

"Ready?" he asked, just as desperate to end this little trip down torture lane. For it was torture to just think about her, let alone be this close to her without touching her.

"I hope so," she said solemnly, and opened her door.

He followed her from the shadows of the parking lot into the low-ceilinged, brightly lit office. He rested his hand against her back as he held the door for her. He both saw and felt her stiffen slightly. Though he knew it was impossible, he was certain he could feel her warmth through her long duster and the clothing she wore beneath it. She raised a shaking gloved hand to weave a strand of her long chestnut hair into the mass slipping from its tether at the back of her head and, in doing so, exposed her long, elegant nape.

He deliberately let the door fall into his back, jabbing his hipbone with the door handle, jarring him free of the impulse to lower his lips to her bare neck, to taste her, to soothe her, or perhaps, selfishly, just to know that he had stolen yet another belated reward.

Corrie felt as if she couldn't breathe. Her body seemed to thrum at the simple touch of his hand on the small of her back. Men touched women there all the time in the West. Every doorway seemed to call for some kind of touch, a finger to an elbow, the cupping of a shoulder. Every walk became an escort accompanied by some archaic and courtly gesture. But when Mack Dorsey placed his hand on her, she felt it to the very deepest part of her. It didn't seem so much a courtesy as a touch of possession, a branding of sorts.

"Miss Stratton?"

"Yes." With a hitching breath, Corrie sidestepped Mack's touch, greeted the gray-haired woman, and approached the front desk.

"I'm Mrs. Jackson. All you have to do is sign these papers right here—and show me some identification, of course—and you can take him with you. He's pretty tired and confused right now. Do you speak Spanish?"

"Yes."

The older woman smiled for the first time. "Oh, good, because Pedro doesn't seem to speak any English. At least, he hasn't so far."

"How long was he here before his mother was missed?" Corrie asked.

"I honestly don't know. We process about one hundred people in a two-hour period on food-stamp day. He could have been here anywhere from one hour to seven. He was hungry, that's for sure. But all he would eat was a candy bar."

"Is he asking for his mother?"

"No, that's the strange part. He seems resigned. Sad, but resigned. It's either happened to him before or he knew it was about to. And such a good little boy, too."

It shouldn't happen to any child, Corrie thought grimly, good or otherwise.

Mrs. Jackson moved to the front doors and inserted a key she turned with a small grunt. "We're closed. Better to be safe than sorry."

Corrie couldn't help but exchange a glance with Mack. She wasn't surprised his jaw tightened. At his next words, however, she realized he wasn't reacting to the same thoughts she was. "You might be locking someone out, but you're also locking us in."

"Pedro might take it in his head to dart out the door and look for his mother. Kids can be amazingly fast little creatures."

"It's a fire hazard," Mack rasped.

Skin grafts for burns, Corrie thought. *Fire burns.*

As quickly as she could, aware Mack was keeping his eyes focused between the keys in Mrs. Jackson's hand and the locked door, Corrie signed the multilayered documents and fished in her purse for her wallet.

As Mrs. Jackson moved to the back to retrieve the little boy, Corrie called Mack's attention from the locked door by simply touching his arm.

"What?" he asked.

"It slays me. All I have to do is sign a piece of paper in triplicate, flash a driver's license, and a scared little six-year-old boy is transferred to my custody. It's harder—and more expensive—to spring a dog from the animal shelter."

Mack gave her an odd look.

"Are you okay?"

He slowly nodded. "I'm fine," he said. And raised a hand to cover the one she'd rested on his forearm.

When Mrs. Jackson—"That's Emily to you, dear"— brought a sleepy Pedro Ortega out of a waiting room, Corrie's chest tightened and her breathing felt constricted. Small even for his young age, the little boy scarcely looked old enough to feed himself, let alone be left on his own. The six-year-old's eyes told a hundred stories of fear and worry as he held back just inside the doorway to study these strangers who had come to take him away.

Memories of her rough childhood burned her mind like acid. A man with hands like granite and the size of boulders had dragged her away from the teary-eyed plump woman who had rocked her so sweetly. The granite hands had proved to be extensions of a rocky

heart and an even more heartless soul. Had she stared
up at him with such worry and fear in young-old eyes?
If so, he hadn't cared.

Her heart wrenched for the little girl she had been
and more for the little boy in front of her. She dropped
down to her knees so as not to tower above the boy.
He shrank back a bit. She settled back on her heels,
hoping to let him know she wasn't as much a threat
as he might imagine.

In the Spanish she'd learned for her global career
and had seldom used to such good effect until she
came to New Mexico, she said, "I'm Corrie. I'm glad
to meet you, Pedro."

When he didn't say anything, she waved a hand up
at Mack. "And this is one of our teachers, Señor
Mack. We live on a big ranch with lots of horses,
puppy dogs and a whole bunch of barn cats. A lot of
other children live there, too. Would you like to come
stay with us for a while until we can find out what
happened to your mother?"

The little boy's eyes slowly studied Corrie, Mack
and Mrs. Jackson.

Mrs. Jackson said, "Miss Stratton, it's not as if he
has any choice—"

"Please, Emily," Corrie interrupted without looking at her, and continued in Spanish to Pedro. "We
have lots of room, good beds and delicious food.
Don't you think so, Mack?"

"The food is one of the best parts," Mack affirmed
in fluent Spanish.

Corrie could have kissed him, not for his Spanish,
but for the support. When she felt his hand drop to her
shoulder, she wanted to close her eyes, to let his touch

flow into her, wrap her in courage. At the same time, the simple gesture inspired a host of noncustodial-type thoughts.

"Rancho Milagro is a great place," Corrie said, resisting the urge to cover Mack's hand with her own. His touch seemed to radiate out from her shoulder, suffusing her with its warmth.

Pedro stood straighter. "Rancho Milagro?" A look of something akin to fear crossed his face. He'd heard of the place, that much was obvious, but what he'd gleaned might not have been good.

"That's right," Corrie said solemnly.

After looking from Corrie to Mack and back to Corrie, the little boy finally summoned the tiniest of smiles.

Corrie withheld her sigh of relief and smiled back at him. "It's a place where we eat miracles for breakfast."

"Sometimes for dinner," Mack added.

Corrie held her breath, not because of the boy, but because of Mack's seemingly casual remark. He inevitably left the table when the children did, avoiding the adult intimacy as if they carried something contagious. Yet now he was telling a scared little boy they ate miracles for dinner. And there was no mistaking the sincerity in his tone.

"So…do you want to come with us?" Corrie asked, taking off her gloves and holding out her bare hand, palm up. Mack's hand on her shoulder gave an encouraging—or warning—squeeze.

A shutter came down over the boy's face and he averted his gaze only to shrug.

"All you have to do for a miracle is to want one," Corrie said. "Wanting one is halfway to getting one."

"No es verdad," Pedro mumbled, but he met her eyes again. Then he added, in Spanish, "There's no such thing as miracles anymore."

"It *is* true," Corrie said. She held out her other hand for Mack's assistance and he took her hand to pull her easily to her feet in a move as smooth as if they'd orchestrated a dance. Did he hold on to her a bit longer than necessary? Or was she the one clinging to his hand?

Pedro looked up at her, then at Mack. The fear and worry still made his young eyes old, but his mouth was less pinched and some of the tension had slipped from his shoulders. He lowered his gaze to Corrie's still outstretched hand. So slowly she actually ached from the anticipation of that little hand in hers, he inched his fingers forward.

Careful not to grip him too fiercely, no granite-hard grasp for this little one, she gently folded her fingers around his. "And Mrs. Jackson will call us the minute she hears any news, won't you, Emily?"

"Yes, of course," the woman said, the relief on her face as evident as the thick makeup. She jingled the keys in her hand. She gave another grunt as she released the lock to free them. "Thank you so much for taking him," she said. "We tried all the usual avenues, but—"

"It's fine, Mrs. Jackson. We're happy to have him," Corrie said in Spanish. The woman had said the little boy didn't speak English though Corrie suspected otherwise. Mrs. Jackson's using English when she was able to speak decent Spanish seemed worse than rude to Corrie, it seemed cruel. "Aren't we, Mack?"

"You bet. The more the merrier." He'd lost at least five years of aging when Emily unlocked the door. He held it for Corrie and Pedro and winked at the little boy as he opened the back door of the Bronco. Light flooded the golden brown interior of the car.

The little fingers in hers convulsed when the boy glimpsed the empty expanse of seat waiting for him.

"It's okay," she said. She passed off his attack of anxiety as concern over being cold. "We have blankets and a pillow for you. And, knowing Rita—she's our cook out at Rancho Milagro—she's packed a little snack for you."

"Want me to help you up?" Mack asked when Pedro still hadn't moved.

"No, *señor*. I can do it." He turned Corrie's hand loose—she could feel how reluctantly—and climbed up the mountain the vehicle must have seemed to him.

"Seat belt," Mack said.

Proving Corrie's suspicions that the boy knew some English, Pedro searched around, found the device and, after some struggling and a warning look at Mack, managed to cinch it around his small frame. Mack shook out a stadium blanket and spread it over the boy, tucking it in so that his face and hands were free but the rest of him was swathed in soft Polartec fleece.

"How's that?" Mack asked.

"Fine, *señor*."

"Hungry?"

Pedro shook his head, but his eyes cut to the picnic basket Mack had placed beside him on the seat.

Mack reached over and flipped the lid open. In

Spanish, he said, "Okay, but if you get that way, all this food was packed just for you. And Rita's feelings get hurt if we don't eat lots and lots of her cooking. There's burritos, a couple of *taquitos,* some cookies— I hope these aren't the ones the other kids made for the puppies, nope, they're the good ones—oh, and I see she put in some milk. Help yourself on the way to the ranch, okay?"

Pedro mumbled a thank-you, his wide eyes on the largesse in the basket.

Mack stepped away from the Bronco, locked it, then shut the back door. "All set," he said, placing his hand at the small of Corrie's back once again to guide her to the driver's seat.

Corrie stared at him for a moment in sheer wonder and wished she were only marginally aware of his touch on her back. He'd made the transfer seem so effortless. She'd only been on one "run" at the ranch thus far and it could only be described as a nightmare. Juan Carlos had pitched a royal fit, had thrown the food out of the window, kicked the blankets aside, bitten Pablo and sullenly refused to talk for the first five hours, unless swearing with uncanny range.

Mack opened the driver's door for her and held his hand out to assist her inside. She felt like Pedro as she hesitated, cautious and hopeful simultaneously, then, slowly placed her palm against his. As she had every time they touched, she felt the shock of contact ripple through her. Inanely she wondered what his silky-soft new hands would feel like against her bare skin.

She used his supporting heft, then, instead of releasing his hand, she added pressure. "Thanks, Mack. You have no idea how much I appreciate your help."

"De nada," he said. He continued to hold her hand.

In English and too softly for Pedro to make out her words, she said, "It wasn't nothing and it means a lot to me."

Mack looked down at their linked hands, lifted hers slightly, and for a moment Corrie half thought he might raise it all the way to his lips. She stilled, both fearing and wanting him to do just that. Instead, he gave her fingers a little squeeze, nothing more than mere reassurance or possibly simple acknowledgement, then released her.

"What you did in there meant a lot to me, too."

"Anybody would want to help a little boy," she said.

He shook his head and lifted a finger to her cheek as if unable to stop himself. "But you also helped a grown man."

Fire burns, she thought.

He drew his finger down her cheek and came to rest on her lips, not as though silencing her, but as if kissing her.

Chapter 7

They weren't past the river and the beautiful surrounding park, when Corrie heard the rustle of tin foil from the back seat. She turned her head slightly, to make sure Pedro was all right and the tinny crackle ceased abruptly.

"When you're ready back there," Mack said, not turning around, "would you get me a cookie? And if you're not going to drink it all, I'll take a little bit of that milk, too."

A few seconds later, Corrie felt a finger tap on her shoulder. "*Señora?* Here's a cookie for the man."

"Thank you, Pedro. Here you go, Mack."

Another silence, broken only by the crunch of cookies breaking.

Lights strafed the highway leading out of Carlsbad, brightening the empty expanse of the road to Roswell. An almost-whisper came from the back seat. "Do you want one, too, *señora?*"

Her heart constricted, but she took a leaf from Mack's seemingly casual concern. "No, thanks. But somebody had better eat mine or Rita will think we don't like them."

"I like them," Pedro said.

"Good. How about the burritos?"

"Are they very hot?"

"No way," Corrie said, understanding the question after several encounters with New Mexico chilies. "Rita wouldn't put too many spices in."

Tinfoil rustled anew and the car was filled with the pungent scent of red chili, cumin and pork and the sound of a hungry young boy eating a late dinner. After a long drink of milk and a satisfied and slightly embarrassed burp, the boy yawned mightily.

On cue, Mack swung around in his seat and shifted the basket to the floor and a pillow to the seat. Once again, he tucked the blanket around the boy, this time covering him for sleep.

Within seconds, the back seat was utterly quiet except for the soft sounds of a tired little boy's rhythmic snoring.

Mack relaxed against the seat. On the way into town, the cab had felt too full of unspoken questions and restless longings. Now, with the addition of a sleeping child, the electricity between them was no less, but the crackling uncomfortable tension had subsided.

Perhaps touching Corrie's back, holding her hand in his had made her seem more approachable, made the chasm he'd created with the kiss the night before seem bridged somewhat, however narrow that passage. Maybe Corrie's awareness of his worry over the locked door, however she may have misinterpreted it, her helping the little boy in the back seat made it seem possible for him to momentarily ignore the nightmare of his past and deal with this woman in the present.

Mack thought about the reasons for a few additional silent miles, then said, "You handled that beautifully."

She flashed him a swift smile. Her face had a greenish glow from the dashboard lights, and strangely, instead of detracting from her beauty, they only seemed to make it seem more ethereal. A pixie of a woman with lush, dark hair, coffee-brown eyes that sparkled in the dark, and hands that had trembled in his and while waiting for a child's timid grasp. Talented and beautiful, fearful and vulnerable. She was a potent mix.

Her grin broadened. "You should have seen me with Juan Carlos."

He chuckled at her description of Juan Carlos's antics at their first encounter. "That kid's a real handful, all right. Trouble is he's smart as a whip."

"Have you noticed that most of them are?"

"Maybe simple survival makes a child use more brainpower."

She pondered that for a moment, silent as she took the turn to the ranch road. "I wonder. That could be true in Leeza's case."

"Leeza? Leeza Nelson?" He couldn't imagine Leeza Nelson ever lacking in survival skills. She was pleasant enough, but her tongue was sharp and her gaze even more so. She looked as if she could chew someone up and spit them out without a backward glance. He was almost amazed she and Corrie were friends; they seemed such opposites.

"Yes. Didn't you know? All three of us are orphans, too."

He hadn't known. No one had told him, then he thought, why would they? It was a confidence and confidences were shared experiences; he didn't exactly hold the corner on revealing inner thoughts and life's experiences.

"We met back in college. We became the sisters we never had. What about you—brothers and sisters?"

"One of each. And two parents, though they're not married to each other anymore."

"I'm sorry."

"Don't be." He almost stopped there, but thought of Corrie's revelation about her past. Remembered the way she'd merely stood there after his brush-off the night before. She deserved more from him. "They're great people, just not with each other. They've both remarried and I like both the new stepparents."

"Where do they live?"

"All of them?"

"All of them."

He told her about his brother's vagabond existence on a research yacht in the Caribbean, his sister's recent marriage to a stockbroker in Idaho, and his parents' lives in northern New Mexico and southern Texas.

He liked the way she listened, interjecting laughter when he solicited it and sympathetic murmurs when he touched on topics that naturally called for empathy.

"How long have you been teaching?"

He stiffened somewhat, dreading the inevitable

questions about his past. "About ten years, give or take."

"You're good at it," she stated, not inviting argument over her pronouncement. "The kids adore you."

He didn't want their adoration or even their trust. He just wanted their safety. Not comfortable with continuing that vein of discussion, he asked, "Why did you leave radio?"

She didn't answer immediately as she was leaving the main highway from Carlsbad to Roswell for the gravel road leading to the ranch. She slowed the Bronco down to avoid swerving and sliding on the rocks.

"Why did I leave PBS? I guess you could call it burnout," she said, making him wonder what *she* called it. "One day it just seemed I'd asked all the questions before. I wasn't editing sound bites for story impact anymore, but because some politico had made a grammatical error."

"Your fans will miss you."

"I doubt that," she said. "There's always some young, starry-eyed kid with a golden voice waiting in the wings somewhere."

"That describes you to a tee."

"I'm no kid anymore."

"You look like one. And, you still have stars in your eyes and a voice that sounds like the low strings of a harp."

He was watching her face and met her look of pleased surprise with a neutrality he hoped let her know he was speaking nothing but the truth. "You said you were an orphan. Were you raised in an orphanage?"

"Mostly, yes," she said, but didn't elaborate.

"Do you want to tell me about it?"

"No," she said firmly, then added, "I'm sorry. But it's long ago and far away and I prefer it to stay that way." She reached a hand out and lightly touched his arm, not looking at him. He wondered if the gesture was to apologize for not sharing her past with him, or to reassure him that she hadn't been broken by it. She was in the process of pulling her hand away when she suddenly dropped it back down, clutching him. "What is *that*?"

Directly ahead of them on the long, lonely ranch road, a figure draped in black walked alone at the edge of the bar ditch.

Mack felt his heart jerk reflexively and his fingertips tingled as adrenaline shot through his system. Everything in him wanted to yell at Corrie to drive faster, to pass the apparition by, because it wasn't of this realm. The figure could only be a ghost.

Corrie braked hard, breathing shallowly. "If I were Catholic, I'd be crossing myself."

The headlights centered on the figure in black, slowly walking down the ranch road in the same direction they had been traveling.

"Tell me you see her, too," she said.

"I see her," he said tersely, though until she'd spoken he hadn't seen the figure as female. Now, because the car was stopped and the headlights shone directly on the phantom, he could make out the long black skirt, the veiled hair and the ghostly pale face turning to look over her shoulder at the car behind her.

"For a minute, I thought she was a ghost," Corrie

said on a breathless little laugh that sounded more
a gasp.

"I have to admit, the hair on my neck is still stick-
ing straight out," Mack said.

The woman in black, alone on a thirty-mile stretch
of empty road, turned away from the car and continued
walking toward the ranch. Again, Mack felt a frisson
of reaction creeping down his spine. Every childhood
ghost story about La Dolorosa's lonely wanderings
flitted through his mind.

"No," he said aloud, then felt foolish as Corrie hesitated in inching the Bronco forward. He felt his face
flush. "I didn't mean stop. I just meant she couldn't
be a ghost."

"You're thinking about La Dolorosa, too, aren't
you?"

He gave a ragged chuckle. "Bingo."

She echoed his laugh but with none of her usual
abandon. She drove the Bronco forward until they
flanked the woman in black. The woman flicked them
a glance from beneath her veil and continued walking.

Corrie nosed the Bronco farther still, pulling to a
stop just a few paces ahead of the woman.

"We have to see what she's doing way out here,"
she said, as if he needed an explanation. "It's freezing.
And supposed to get colder before dawn."

Mack lowered his window, glanced at the back seat
to make sure Pedro was still sleeping, then called out
softly in Spanish, "Are you okay, *señora?*"

The woman approached the window at the same
even pace she'd been employing before. As she got
closer, Mack again suffered a pang of doubt. Would
she prove real?

Corrie felt shivers of superstition working their way up her spine. A woman walking the ranch road, thirty miles north of Carlsbad, was impossible enough. Dressed all in black on a fitful night in an unseasonably cold spring, the woman sparked a whole universe of fears that had lived deep within the little girl Corrie had once been.

"Can we help you, *señora?*" Mack asked.

The woman shook her head.

"Did your car break down?" It was a patently ridiculous question; they'd have seen such a vehicle.

The woman shook her head again. Her dark eyes fathomless and unreadable, she looked into the back seat of the Bronco. She stared at the sleeping child beneath the blanket.

To Mack, her eyes looked hungry.

"Do you need a ride?" Mack offered. Say no, he pleaded silently. Just shake your veiled head and disappear into the night.

The woman moved to the back door and reached for the handle. Her hands seemed ghostly pale, then, as she extended one, tinged with red in the glow cast by the taillights.

Corrie couldn't stop herself from reaching out for Mack's shoulder. Whether she'd intended to stop him from unlocking the door, or simply for human contact, she didn't know. All she understood was the need to feel his solid male body.

Mack threw her a quick glance, then lifted the lock on the rear door, and swung it open. Amber light spilled across the woman's angular features, softening them as she stared in at the boy snoring softly. In the light, Corrie could see the woman hadn't been wearing a black funereal veil, but had simply pulled her long woolen shawl up and around her head. She lowered it now, drawing it tightly around her neck, and lifted her long black skirt to step into the car.

She closed the door after her and stiffly sat back against the seat, apparently careful not to disturb the child beside her.

Corrie envisioned Jeannie and Leeza mourning at a three-way funeral. Jeannie would ask why their friend would pick up a hitchhiker when she had a little boy in the car. Leeza would shake her head and say the police said they couldn't find a weapon; they'd all apparently died of fright.

But the woman staring straight ahead didn't seem menacing. While Corrie could feel the cold emanating from her, the chill of a May night in the desert southwest, she didn't feel a threat other than to her sanity.

When several seconds had passed and Corrie still hadn't released the foot brake, the woman's eyes cut to hers and away.

Corrie gulped air and fought to stifle the hysterical giggles that threatened to escape. Mack clasped her hand and she almost screamed. Until he took her hand in his, she hadn't realized she was still clutching his shoulder.

"I thought you were a ghost," Corrie said.

The woman said nothing.

"I thought you were La Dolorosa."

The woman remained silent.

"It's okay. Let's just drive," Mack murmured. He moved her hand to the gearshift knob, as if she wouldn't have been able to do it without his aid. In that, he was probably correct for she had to think for a moment how to engage the car.

She looked in the rearview mirror at the woman in back. She'd half expected to see an empty seat, as the ghost stories went, but the woman was there, eyes forward and her thin, pale lips silently moving.

Long-buried memories eddied in Corrie. Every ghost story told at the orphanage, a flashlight in the teller's hand, girls huddled beneath a blanket to hide from the light, seemed to coalesce and re-form right in the Bronco. In almost every country and certainly in most states of the United States, a woman in black walked the back roads and country lanes. Known by a variety of names, she wailed in one place, was silent in another.

In Carlsbad and other parts of the southwest, she was known as La Dolorosa, the Woman of Sorrow, who walked the lonely roads in search of her missing children. According to Rita, whenever she came, bad luck followed in her wake.

Corrie whispered, "I am Corrie Stratton. And if I survived my childhood, I can survive anything." She slowly eased the car into first, then second, and finally took them up to as normal a speed as nighttime driving on a dirt road allowed.

Pedro made some sound, and before Mack could reach over the seat, the woman in the back had adjusted the blanket and was patting the boy's shoulder. The child sighed deeply and went back to sleep.

Corrie fought the shiver that worked its way over her. She risked a glance at Mack. He was sitting cantilevered in his seat, one arm over the back, and she knew the pose rendered him swift to protect Pedro.

They drove some ten miles in unnatural silence, then the woman tapped on Mack's shoulder and pointed to her door.

"What? You want us to stop?"

Corrie complied without having to be asked.

The woman reached for the door.

"Wait," Mack said. "You can't get out here. There's nothing but empty field out there."

The woman shook her head and pointed to what amounted to a dirt track off the main ranch road.

"That's just a feeding station road," Corrie said. "It doesn't go anywhere." But she shuddered. The road actually did go past the crumbling ruins of an adobe dwelling. She'd seen it while out riding with Pablo one afternoon.

The woman pointed at the road again, with greater determination. She pulled the handle and the Bronco door swung open, letting in a blast of cold air.

"Wait, *señora,*" Corrie called. "You'll freeze to death out there. Come with us to the ranch. You'll be safe there." But would the ranch be safe with her?

The woman ignored her, stepping down from the car. She turned and looked squarely at Corrie. Her eyes conveyed a plea and an apology of sorts. She pointed down the dirt track at a right angle to the ranch road, then adjusted her long shawl, lifting it over her hair and tossing one end over her shoulder.

She shut the door gently and turned her back on the car. She'd walked maybe four or five steps before Corrie threw the Bronco into Park and hurled herself from the vehicle.

"Wait!"

The woman stopped and half turned. She held herself perfectly still as Corrie rushed up to her.

"Take these," Corrie said, thrusting her gloves at the woman. "And this." She shrugged out of her duster and handed it to the stranger. The woman shook her head, but Corrie was insistent. Finally, ghostly pale hands reached for the proffered items.

The woman slung the coat around her shoulders like a cape and slowly pulled on the leather, fur-lined gloves. She nodded and turned her back on the car. Within seconds, the inky-black desert swallowed up her equally dark figure.

Stung by cold, worried about the woman, confused by the night, Corrie ran back to the car and climbed back up. She shut the door, cranked the heat a notch higher and put the car in reverse. She backed up and positioned the car so the headlights would shine down the dirt track. The lights easily picked out the steady walk of the woman in black.

"I don't feel right about this," Corrie said.

"She wanted out. Who knows what's going on, but she was pretty adamant about getting out at this track."

"But there's nothing out there."

"Nothing we know about."

"What does that mean?" Corrie asked, afraid she knew exactly.

Mack ran a hand through his short hair. "I don't know. Nothing, probably. Maybe somebody's waiting down the road for her. A husband. A lover. Who knows?"

"At least she has gloves and a coat."

"You're a Good Samaritan."

"Or I just gave Leeza's three-hundred-dollar gift to a ghost."

"And the rest of the food."

"The food? She stole it?"

"All that was left."

"At least Rita won't have hurt feelings."

"At least."

"Mack…do you suppose…?"

"No. At least, no, I don't think she's La Dolorosa, if that's what you were going to ask."

Corrie looked at him.

"Let's go," he said. "We've done all we can. Pablo and the crew can come look for her tomorrow. For now we have Pedro to think about."

"You're right," she said, but she didn't put the car in first gear yet. "But you have to admit it's weird."

"Oh, it's way beyond weird."

Corrie giggled. "I really thought she was a ghost."

"You weren't the only one. I was making the sign against the evil eye the whole time she was in the car."

Corrie laughed outright at that image and used young José's favorite line. "I almost screamed like a *girl*."

"Me, too," Mack said, and to her delight, he began to laugh. It shook free of him like an avalanche, rumbling and deep, forceful and strong.

After a moment of sheer wonder, she laughed with him, leaning forward, resting her forehead on his shoulder. And suddenly she was aware he wasn't laughing anymore. She raised her eyes to his and her own slightly hysterical giggles cut off as abruptly as they had started.

She read too many conflicting messages in his eyes, but as he lifted a hand to her face, she understood one meaning with crystal clarity. Her heart beat like a timpani in her chest. She tilted her head and felt her lips parting of their own volition.

The groan that escaped him sounded as if it came from some tortured part of him, but she answered it with a whispered and inchoate plea.

He pulled her closer, his hands roughly drawing her to him, his lips capturing hers with rough and almost desperate passion.

Whatever fear she'd felt upon seeing the figure in black coalesced into a fear of another sort, a fear and an almost inexplicable sense of rightness. It seemed her lips recognized his, her body remembered his. And the sensation, instead of reducing her reaction to him, only served to increase it. She felt as though she'd always been hungry and had now been given a taste of some perfect, heretofore unknowable food. And it made her crave another taste and then another.

After a few eons of time, he raised his head and pulled at the warm air inside the Bronco as if he'd never drawn oxygen before. His hand against her cheek shook and he stared at her as if she'd burst into flames in his arms.

It wasn't far from the truth. Until the night before, and only with him, had she ever experienced such turbulent passion. The ardor felt simultaneously hot and cold, painful and healing, and left her the impression that it was something forbidden, something that Mack risked now but might never attempt again. It carried the seeds of promise and was spiced with the already bitter herbs of goodbye.

He pulled back, and though she would have given anything to continue to feel his embrace, she was too confused by it herself, too easily bruised afterward to plead with him for more, and too aware of the sleeping child in the back seat. She slowly straightened, dazed nearly witless and completely forgetful of the woman in black.

Almost instinctively, she held her hands out in front of her. They weren't trembling. As they hadn't after Mack had kissed her the night before. When his lips had pressed to hers, her heart had never beat quite as irregularly, her breath had never been threadier, and yet her hands were rock steady, as calm as a surgeon's.

As far as she knew, her hands had started shaking when she was in grade school. The doctors her various foster parents had taken her to had shaken their heads and claimed genetics as the source, and named the strange phenomenon "familial tremors." But no tests had ever been done. And if they had, would the cure have included Mack Dorsey's kisses?

Numbly, she once again put the car in gear and resumed their journey to the ranch. When they saw the lights of the ranch in the far distance, still some two miles from their present location, Mack cleared his throat. "Corrie."

"Yes?" Was her voice really as breathless as it sounded in her own ears?

"I'm sorry. I—"

"Don't apologize," she murmured. "Please." How could he apologize for something so incredible?

"I don't want—"

Tears stung her eyes. Only a couple of hours earlier, she would have given almost anything if only he would speak. Now she felt any words he might say would crush her completely. "Please," she asked again. "Let's just get inside."

He acceded to her wishes, and after a few seconds she glanced over at him. He was staring straight ahead, his jaw rigid. She jerked her eyes forward.

His gravelly voice ground out, "The hell of it is, I've been wanting to kiss you for years."

"Years?" she asked, truly startled.

"Ever since I first heard you on the radio."

"Oh." He'd succeeded in confusing her even further.

"It can't happen again," he said. "It would be unfair to you."

Corrie didn't say anything. She didn't know how to ask why not, the way Leeza would have, or assure him that she understood, as Jeannie might have done. She didn't understand and didn't have the courage to demand an explanation. As she often did, she cursed her own lack of courage. It had driven her from the only career she'd ever known, countless opportunities, and now prevented her from asking a man who had just kissed her as if there were no tomorrow why he said it couldn't happen again. When she knew he wanted it as badly as she did.

She negotiated the turn into Rancho Milagro's large open gates, numbed to the joy she usually felt upon arriving at her new home. She punched the gate lock's automatic button with a now shaking finger.

"You said you were looking for a miracle," he said.

She couldn't remember saying that. She remembered agreeing with him when he said *he* wanted to be a part of what Milagro was about. She stilled herself for more.

"Believe me when I tell you that I'm about the furthest thing from a damned miracle."

She gripped her hands on the steering wheel, wanting to rail at him, wanting to throw the car into Park and turn on him, demanding where he got off making such assumptions about her—about himself. But she wasn't made that way. She was the person who always sat on the sidelines, reporting the incidents, never taking a place in them. She was the one who never made waves, never fought, because words could change a life in a heartbeat and change it for the worse.

She pulled the car up to the front door of the hacienda and slowly put the car into Park. She drew the emergency brake almost idly.

"Do you understand?" he asked.

She turned to look at him then, unaccustomed anger fanning through her. "Not one little bit," she said curtly, and secretly relished the astonishment on his chiseled features. So he would find out what no one else ever had before, that sweet little Corrie Stratton, who never argued, never grumbled, and never, ever fought, had a bite lurking somewhere inside her.

"Will you help me with Pedro?"

"I—sure," he said, exiting the car as if she might strike out at him.

Corrie yanked the back door open, drew a deep breath, then much more gently unbuckled the seat belt holding Pedro inside. She nudged the boy's shoulder to wake him. He didn't stir.

"Let me," Mack said.

Corrie stepped back without a word.

"Come on, little guy, let's get you inside." He hefted the boy to his shoulder and cradled him against his broad chest.

Corrie thought about how it had felt to lay her head against that same chest, how she'd heard his heart beating so rapidly, how it seemed to thunder in her ear. She thought about how right it had felt to be enveloped in his arms.

The door to the hacienda opened and Jeannie stepped out on the veranda. "Good. We were just getting worried. Where's your coat, honey? Did something happen?"

Corrie stepped around Mack. "I gave my coat to a ghost and kissed Mack. He can tell you the rest."

Chapter 8

Corrie tried escaping to her room as Pedro was installed in one of the many bedrooms, but Mack grabbed her arm. "Wait just a minute," he said. His eyes were shards of ice.

"No, thanks," she said, pulling her arm free of his grasp. She was dimly aware that had he been determined to hold her; nothing short of dynamite could have freed her. She refused to meet his gaze though she felt him silently compelling her to do so.

Jeannie stepped into the living room and, after a strangely cautious glance at Corrie and a speculative one at Mack, went to the side table and asked Rita to pour out two mugs of chocolate. "Mack, would you build up the fire?"

A tight-lipped Mack complied as Jeannie handed a mug to Corrie. With his back turned, he couldn't have seen the sharp question in Jeannie's eyes.

Corrie took it gratefully, her fingers cold after being outside without gloves, her heart even colder still. She shook her head at her friend.

Jeannie sat down on one of the large sofas. "What's this about your coat?"

Corrie turned her back to the room. Her brief but heartfelt spurt of anger was fading too rapidly. Already, guilt and the horror of being rude were overtaking it. She couldn't have spoken if her life depended on it.

Mack rescued her, saying, "On the way back from Carlsbad, we came across a woman walking alone on the ranch road."

"*Dios mio,*" Rita said. Corrie pictured the tiny woman crossing herself. "La Dolorosa. I knew it! She's here."

Corrie shook her head and looked at the ceiling. She couldn't help but recall the way Mack's laughter had rumbled in the car, had felt against her cheek.

He gave a jagged chuckle. "That's what we thought, too, at first. I have to admit, it wasn't hard to think it. She was dressed all in black, complete with a black shawl over her head. But she was real enough. We gave her a ride."

Rita moaned. "The bad luck comes. You should never have given her a ride. Don't tell me, she wasn't there when you got out of the car."

Corrie took a sip of her chocolate and winced as the hot liquid burned her mouth.

Behind her, Jeannie asked, "Where is she now?"

"She wanted off on what Corrie said was a feeding-station track."

Corrie could almost hear Jeannie's frown. "Did she say what she was doing out this way?"

"She didn't say anything at all," Corrie said, turning around, looking anywhere but at Mack. "She only nodded or shook her head. Or tapped Mack on the shoulder when she wanted to stop. Then she pointed at the feeding-station track."

Rita crossed herself. "The ruins…"

"She wasn't a ghost," Mack repeated. "She stole the food Pedro didn't eat."

"A hungry ghost. I haven't heard too many stories about those," Jeannie said mildly. "But I think I'd better call Chance and have him look for her on his way home." She consulted her watch. "That'll be in about a half an hour."

"I gave her my coat and gloves," Corrie offered. "I felt terrible just leaving her out there. But short of wrestling her back into the car, we didn't have much choice."

"I suppose Chance could arrest her for trespassing on private property. But you're right, shy of kidnapping her, if she doesn't want to come, we don't have much power to force her into coming in where it's warm," Mack said.

"I don't want to think about some poor woman dying of exposure out on the ranch somewhere," Jeannie said.

"She has Corrie's coat and gloves. And it's not even going to frost tonight, even though the windchill is mean as hell," Mack said. "I'll go out in the morning before lessons."

"Or Chance can—no, he can't. We're heading out tomorrow."

"Pablo and I can go," Corrie suggested.

"No, he can't. He and Clovis are scheduled to round up the strays in the Guadalupes," Jeannie said. She didn't look at Corrie as she concluded, "Looks like it will have to be the two of you again."

Corrie could have cheerfully shot her dearest friend.

"Unless Chance finds her tonight and persuades her to come in."

"And you won't look until the daylight," Rita said.

"In the daylight," Jeannie agreed.

"Fine, then," Mack said tersely. "For now, I'd better get some sleep." He handed his mug back to Jeannie. "Thanks for the cocoa."

He leveled an inscrutable look at Corrie on his way by. She met it impassively, fighting the urge to apologize, warring with the need to erase her reckless comment to Jeannie about his kissing her, knowing she couldn't do either.

"Sleep well," she said, then felt bad about saying it, knowing he wouldn't, that he never did. She managed to get to her bedroom and put her head beneath her pillow before the front door even closed behind him.

She'd learned early that temper only created chaos. She'd had it hammered into her that an angry person was the only one with cause to apologize. Keeping one's temper in check meant one possessed a clear mind and a kind heart. And all those adages had proved true throughout her adolescent years.

The quieter she was, the less difficulty she had anywhere she was placed. *She's a quiet little thing. She's a good, biddable little girl. I'll say this for her, she never argued with us. She never caused us any embarrassment.*

Not ten minutes later, still groaning into her pillow, she heard Jeannie's knock and the creak of the door opening. "I called Chance. He's going to drive out that way and see if he can find her."

"Good," Corrie said from beneath her protective pillow.

"Want to talk about it?"

"No."

"Liar," Jeannie said, coming into the room and closing the door behind her. Less than a minute later, Leeza did the same. They both sat on Corrie's bed, just as they'd done a thousand times in college and off and on during the years after. Had Jeannie consulted Leeza or had the astute woman just known something was up?

"So, what's this I hear about you kissing Mack Dorsey?" Leeza asked.

Corrie moaned.

"That's what I like," Leeza said mildly, "the short version, no gory details."

Corrie couldn't help but chuckle. However, she didn't remove the pillow.

"How did he make you mad?" Jeannie asked.

"By telling me it wouldn't happen again," Corrie said, and had to repeat herself after lifting the pillow. She felt every kind of a fool.

"And I take it you want it to happen again?"

"No. Yes. I don't know."

Corrie sensed her friends' exchange of glances. She felt Jeannie's gentle hand on her back. "Don't worry about it."

"I'm so embarrassed."

"About what? That Corrie Stratton actually kissed a man?" Leeza asked.

"No. Well, a little. But mainly because I got mad at him because he hurt my feelings. And then I snapped at him."

"Guess what, Corrie, it's about damned time you snapped at something. You're years behind in that department," Leeza said mildly. "You've always been so busy trying to be a wallflower that you never even noticed that you're the belle of the ball."

When Corrie didn't say anything, Leeza added, "Of course, we can't fire him now."

Corrie twisted around and sat up, shoving her hair off her face. "Who said anything about firing him?"

"I'm glad you agree. That would smack of sexual harassment. We are his employers, you know. It's not really kosher to go around kissing the hired help and then firing them."

"For heaven's sake," Corrie sputtered. "He's not hired help. He's—he's already indispensable around here. The kids would fall apart if he left."

Leeza chuckled and flicked her cheek with a long, tapered finger. "So make him eat his words…and make him stay. And, whatever you do, don't apologize for getting angry at him. If anything, thank him. It's a Corrie Stratton first."

Mack woke as he always did, with the screams of children echoing in his ears.

His first night on the ranch, Corrie had warned him about ghosts. And just that night they'd both thought they'd seen one. But Mack knew Corrie thought in terms of wraiths, ghostly figures on lonely roads, a wailing woman seeking her lost children.

She didn't know the first thing about real ghosts. He'd lived with them daily for the past two years. They haunted his every step, his every breath, and screamed when and if he finally managed to fall asleep.

He washed down a couple of aspirin with a gulp of the mineral-heavy liquid that passed for water on Rancho Milagro. Slowly the agonized sound of children's cries faded from his mind, not disappearing but recessing into the background, ready to come forward again anytime he closed his eyes or let his thoughts drift for a while.

Luckily, he had these children at Rancho Milagro to think about now, living children to concentrate on. And Corrie to try ignoring. The trouble was, if he thought about these new children for any length of time, the faces of the other children would steal in, looking at him with accusation and hurt. Betrayal.

The bigger trouble was that thinking about Corrie seemed to keep thoughts of those doomed children at bay, but thoughts about her were every bit as torturous as the ones he had of the lost children. Without any need to focus his attention on her, he could still taste her, smell her fresh scent and drown in her giving touch.

What would be the harm of just taking what she seemed to so readily offer? She wanted him as much as he wanted her. He knew that with every fiber of his being. But it would be like plucking a rare flower and leaving it without water. He could sense the depth of the woman-child within her and refused to be a party to hurting her. And hurt her he would.

The magic of holding her first stiff, then compliant body against his was just what the doctor ordered. But he couldn't bear it if she knew what he'd done. He didn't know which would be worse, if she, like so many other misguided souls, would consider him a hero, or if—as he did—she might damn him for the lost lives.

And yet, after having tasted her, felt what a marvel it was to hold her in his arms, he physically hurt from the longing to repeat it, to just tell her about his past and have her understanding. If her voice was like the sound of paradise, her touch was a healing hand to soothe his brow and her kiss a promise of hope.

But he didn't believe in promises. God knew, he'd made too many two years ago and had lied to every single child he'd lost. If he continued the path he'd been unable to resist with Corrie, she would soon learn about the scars she couldn't see, the wounds imperfectly healed.

He'd seen her light burning late into the night. He'd seen the shadows beneath her eyes the following day. And he'd heard the puzzled pain in her voice when she'd asked him not to apologize when he'd tried telling her they couldn't repeat a kiss that seemed to strike at the very center of his soul.

And he couldn't offer her the reasons why it had to be that way. He could tell her about himself, his past, and the horror that lingered inside him, but it wouldn't explain the nightmares, wouldn't begin to cover the deep well of guilt that dogged him every single day, and would only partially let her glimpse the face of the man he'd been before. Or, making him feel more uncomfortable, the man she almost made him want to be again.

He turned off his light and sat for a while in the darkness, staring across the expanse of grounds at the brightly lit window that separated her from him. Why did she sleep with the light on? And if she wasn't sleeping, what kept such peace at bay?

And what about that unexpected flare of temper? She'd been right to be angry, and right to call him on it. It had just surprised him. He hadn't heard an angry note in her voice the entire time he'd been on the ranch. *When Corrie Stratton says it's true, it's a fact.*

And how could he sit in a car with her the next morning and not drag her into his arms again and kiss her as senseless as she made him?

Nevertheless, shortly after dawn, after a hurried conversation with Chance and hearing that the marshal hadn't seen so much as a sign of the woman in black, he joined Corrie at the Bronco.

Her eyes skittered to his, only to veer off to his shoulder. She was wearing a thick woolen poncho and tall leather boots that somehow made her look like a kid dressed up in her mother's clothes, instead of the strong ranch woman the clothing implied. Her glorious hair was caught up in its usual twist-cum-ponytail and her darkened eyes told the story of a night as restless as his own.

"Would you mind driving this time?" she asked. "I want to watch out for her."

He refrained from pointing out that she was a lot more familiar with the ranch roads, merely holding the passenger door open for her. She shied away from his proffered hand and he pulled it back as if she'd slapped him.

Once behind the wheel, he all but ground the gears, forcing the car to do his frustrated bidding.

"This shouldn't take long. We'll either find her and talk her into coming back to the ranch, or have to send someone out to take her into town." she said.

He was vaguely surprised she was talking to him at all and was grateful that she'd picked an utterly neutral topic. "Unless she was a ghost," he said with a slight smile. "Chance didn't find her and he wasn't too far behind us."

When she merely responded with a faint and wholly distant smile of her own, he asked, "Is there really an abandoned place there?"

"Really."

"A ranch house?"

"Or something. It's mostly ruined walls and an old fireplace now, adobe, what's left of a couple of mud walls."

Mack felt like grinding his teeth. He'd wanted neutral, had hoped for it. Now that he had it, he wanted to shatter it, break through her reserve and talk about the night before. He had to bite back an apology for his words following the kiss. He'd been speaking nothing but the truth, and yet, because he wanted her so badly it hurt, he'd done the one thing he hadn't wanted to and caused her pain.

Her reaction wasn't too tough to figure out. It didn't take a rocket scientist. Rejection was a tough call at any time, and minutes after a mind-shattering kiss, it was the cruelest act of all.

"Corrie—"

"There's the track," she said, cutting him off.

He almost flipped the car, taking the turn so abruptly onto the narrow dirt track.

"Now, around this next curve we should hit an arroyo. After that, the ruins."

Mack didn't say anything, forcing the car to stay on the rough excuse for a road.

As she'd said, after the washed-out arroyo, they cleared a rise and below lay the abandoned half structure of a former small home. He pulled to a halt beside what was left of it.

Everything about the place spoke of emptiness. No birds called, no trees, even denuded by winter, lingered around the place. Even the brisk breeze that had been blowing earlier seemed to avoid this shallow valley.

"Corrie—"

"She can't be here," Corrie interrupted, and, despite her assertion, climbed out of the car.

Mack swore beneath his breath but followed suit. When Corrie would have stepped through the remnants of what had once been a doorway, he deliberately held out his hand and moved in front of her. He walked beneath a leaning lintel held upright by a couple of strips of charred wood. A fire had taken this place down, he thought, his heart scudding in his chest. He could hear the faint wail of children crying for help.

He kept his hand outstretched to keep Corrie from following until he could make certain the place was indeed empty. And safe.

To his left he could see the crumbled remains of a fireplace and an adjacent wall. These bits of a former house stood like a triangular gravestone in the middle of a rectangle of desolation.

"She's not here," Corrie repeated in a near whisper.

"No," Mack agreed, though his eyes were locked on something bundled in the corner beside the fireplace. "But she's been here. I can see why Chance didn't see this last night."

"What is that?" Corrie asked, her hand curving around his arm, much as she'd done the night before. Her touch sent a shock wave through him, making him draw a harsh breath.

"I believe it's your coat," Mack said through a constricted throat.

Corrie waited while Mack retrieved her coat and gloves. He shook them out before handing them to her.

"They're cold," she said. "She must have left them behind first thing this morning."

Mack didn't say anything, his back rigid and his face grim. His icy eyes were focused on the dirt floor of the ruin.

"What is it?" Corrie asked, but even as she questioned him, she knew what he was looking at. His footsteps were clearly visible in the early morning light—a set of Saucony tennis shoe prints going to the corner to retrieve her coat and a matching set coming back. No other marks disturbed the many layers of silt and sand.

She stretched out her own boot and pressed it into the ground, much more lightly than she would have trod. She pulled it back. A perfect toe print marred the earth floor.

An atavistic sense of wrongness gripped Corrie, and she wanted to toss the expensive duster and gloves that

Leeza had given her to the ground. A dimly held precept that one didn't deliberately throw away good things or gifts was all that kept the items in her hands.

"She could have walked around behind the walls."

"Yes," Corrie said with a little more enthusiasm than the suggestion warranted. "That would explain it. The lack of footprints."

"She could have just tossed them there, figuring we would come looking for her in the morning."

"Or she could have had a car waiting for her outside the walls and just dropped them there."

"Any of those things are possible," Mack said.

"Anything's possible."

"Like for you to forgive me for last night?" His voice, deepened by emotion, seemed to slice through her. Her eyes cut to his and the rough demand in his blue eyes snared her completely. She must have looked confused because he added, "For the stupid things I said?"

"I should apologize, too—"

"No," he said firmly, taking a step forward. "You had every right to be angry. You've been nothing but wonderful from day one. I'm the one who's been slinging a bushel full of mixed signals."

"You were pretty clear last night," she said. Her voice felt rusty, her jaw stiff.

"Yes, if you mean my wanting to kiss you. And liking it. And wanting to do it again."

"You do?"

"God, yes," he said, and reached out as if he would touch her face, only to pull his hand back and drag it through his hair instead.

Every instinct in Corrie told her to retreat, to be

silent, to literally leave well enough alone. Every adage she'd been raised with clamored at her to let her gaze fall from his and just walk away. *All's well that ends well—Shakespeare. Can one go upon hot coals and his feet not be burned?—Proverbs. If you can't take the heat, get out of the kitchen—some crazed coward.*

"Please kiss me, then," she said. Her heart beat a jagged rhythm in her chest; her breathing seemed tangled in her throat. She suspected her hands were shaking and knew full well her knees were. And yet she continued to stand exactly where she was, her eyes linked with his, her request hanging in the air between them. "Please."

Even if he drew her into the hell he lived, even if he hurt her immeasurably in the far distant next ten minutes, Mack could no more have resisted Corrie's request than he could have stopped himself from running into that burning hallway two years ago.

The two feet separating them disappeared in a single step forward. He plunged a trembling hand into her amazing hair and used the other to sweep the coat and gloves from her grasp and draw her body to his. As his lips lowered onto hers, capturing her very breath, he told himself to stop, to hold back, to remember the myriad reasons he shouldn't be giving in to this fierce demand. But as her lips opened to him, as her hand stole around his neck to pull him even closer, all rational thought evaporated.

He was a man and she was every man's dream of a woman. And in a force as primal as tides, moonrises, and as turbulent as hurricanes and thunderstorms, he lost himself in the wonder of holding her close, tasting her, drinking in her scent, drowning in her moans of acceptance.

Corrie felt awash in contrasting sensations. An icy breeze teased at her fingers while Mack's fiery-hot lips sparked a raging fire within her. She seemed mindless, yet had never thought more clearly in her life. As his hands tangled in her hair, making her moan with a wanton lust, she understood how long she'd been standing on the outside of life. Maybe it took feeling fire to know it could burn. Maybe it took tasting a man's unbridled hunger to know how to give it in return.

His free hand roamed her back, then slid beneath her warm poncho. She gasped as his cold fingers grasped her body and sighed when they created a blaze in her loins. Her already trembling knees gave way, and it seemed she was floating in his rock-hard grip.

If La Dolorosa had led them there, if she was an apparition only of lonely nights, then she'd blessed them by abandoning them by day, leaving this place empty of all but a thick duster and a pair of gloves.

As if reading her thoughts, Mack groaned aloud and lowered her to the duster he'd spilled to the ground. Like a magician, he swung it open, creating a bed with a wave of his hand.

He cushioned her head in the crook of his arm and gently swept her hair from her face. Cold fingers—hot touch.

"Corrie…"

"Please," she said, unable to voice anything else but sheer want, utter need.

"Look at me, Corrie," he whispered.

She felt as if she heard his voice from far away, his

The Editor's "Thank You" Free Gifts Include:

- 1 Harlequin Intrigue® book!
- 1 Silhouette Intimate Moments® book!
- An exciting mystery gift!

PLACE FREE GIFT SEAL HERE

Yes I have placed my Editor's "Thank You" seal in the space provided above. Please send me 2 FREE books and a fabulous Mystery Gift. I understand I am under no obligation to purchase any books, as explained on the back and on the opposite page.

389 HDL DU3G   189 HDL DU3Q

FIRST NAME   LAST NAME

ADDRESS

APT.#   CITY

STATE/PROV.   ZIP/POSTAL CODE

(H-SA-05/03)

Thank You!

touch already having taken her as far from earthly ground as possible.

He was bent over her, his eyes clouded with want, his lips moist with her kisses. "You make me crazy," he said.

"Welcome to the nuthouse," she quipped, and was amazed at how naturally the light banter slipped from her tongue. A minor miracle.

He swept her poncho up and it pooled around her neck. He lifted her slightly and slipped it from her head, letting it become a pillow. His hot gaze burned through her thin layer of clothing, heating her.

He said raggedly, "Corrie, if you want to stop, tell me now. Because God knows in half a second there won't be any turning back."

"If you stop now, I'd probably die right here," she murmured, and thought that in another place or time she might have blushed at her own temerity. As it was, she reached for his jacket and slid her hands into the warm interior, making him draw a sharp breath.

"I don't have protection," he rasped.

Corrie couldn't help the rush of desire his simple words brought her, nor hide the sudden flare of color in her cheeks.

He lowered his lips to the pulse throbbing just above her collarbone. He deftly unbuttoned her blouse, spreading her blouse open, and ran the tips of his fingers across the swell of her breasts.

"In—in the pocket of my duster," she gasped out.

He gave a rough chuckle, his hot breath fanning her breasts. "Prepared?"

She squirmed beneath his touch, his fire-kissed lips. "I'm—I'm the sex education teacher."

He gave a muffled chortle in the hollow between
her breasts. "They must love your classes."

She answered his chuckle with a gasp as his hand
freed a breast from the confines of her bra and his
fingers took a hardened nipple in a swift, sure capture.

Molten liquid coursed through her and she arched
upward, her hands automatically seeking his face to
draw him down to her.

"This should be a bed on a moonlit night," he said.

"This is perfect," she said, and gently caught his
lower lip between her teeth.

Mack drew in his breath on a hiss. It did seem perfect. His every fantasy come true. And, thrusting con-
science and good intentions aside, he couldn't resist
seizing the perfection and damning the inevitable shoe
falling later. The result might very well be a terrifying
plummet into chaos, but for this moment, in this time,
the touch of her hand, the feel of her lips against his
drove consequences to some nether region.

When her fingers dipped inside his shirt, making
contact with the damaged skin on his chest, he had to
close his eyes against succumbing too rapidly to the
sheer pleasure of being touched, of being caressed.
Her sigh of pleasure made him want to pull her even
closer, plunge into her and just stay there forever, lose
himself in a perfect world that held no nightmares, no
fires, no dying children.

And yet, as she spread open his shirt, her heavy-
lidded eyes taking in the evidence of his past, he felt
burned anew by her touch, by her nonjudgmental,
steady gaze.

"Does it hurt?" she asked.

More than you can ever know, he wanted to tell

her. "No," he said, because truthfully, her touch, while enflaming him, didn't cause physical pain.

"You feel new," she murmured.

He stilled. With her, he *felt* new. Renewed. Reborn. As if promises and hope were possible. As though right around a touch he would find that miracle he'd sought when coming to the ranch.

"And you feel like a wonder," he said, exploring her, tasting what he discovered.

She did feel wonder as his hands brought her body alive. Hunger, impatience and longing rippled through her, followed by waves of slow, almost painful enticement as his fingers danced and plied, teased and tortured.

She couldn't have guessed when her body was bared to his gaze, for it seemed to her that her clothes magically evaporated. But once they were removed, she was heated by the harsh need in his hungry eyes.

"You're so incredibly lovely," he said. As if he were an artist, he brushed her bare breasts with his fingertips. Like a sculptor, he molded them to his hands, kneading, reshaping, then using his tongue on her nipples.

Like a musician, he played symphonies on her skin, creating a sweet harmony of his breath and hers. His tongue danced and played while his fingers created a counterpoint harmony. His hands exhorted while his body pressed against hers.

And when she would have screamed aloud, begging him, ordering him to take her, he dug into her duster pockets and unerringly found the packets he sought.

"I wondered what you had in your pockets that

night you came to the bunkhouse,'' he said, tearing open a packet with his teeth.

She chuckled, relishing the sound, stretching out beneath him, reaching for his male hardness. He bounced in her hands, like an eager animal, then grew even larger in her capture.

''They were probably there then, too.''

''Good thing I didn't know it,'' he murmured before kissing her fiercely.

He sheathed himself with the condom, gripping her hands as he rolled it downward, helping her slip it over his length. Then, while she still held him warm in her grasp, he slid a finger inside her. And back out. And inside again.

''Mack…''

Instead of answering, he bent over her and trapped her lips beneath his. His tongue slipped into her mouth as his finger slipped into her core and he rocked into her hands.

She dragged her lips free. ''Oh, please. Please.'' But she didn't know what she was begging him for.

Mack felt crazed with the need to join Corrie, to unite in the most primitive of ways. She lay open beneath him, her magnificent eyes at half-mast. Her hands pulled him to her, demanding, imploring.

As he hadn't been able to resist her before, not even the reappearance of La Dolorosa could make him do so now. Half fearing what entering would make him feel if just touching her made him so alive, he lowered himself into her.

''Corrie,'' he ground out as he slid into her warm sheath of pure liquid fire.

He felt her rise to meet him, as if they'd been to

gether a thousand times instead of this first. She shuddered and cried out his name as he continued into her, impaling her beneath him. Her legs encircled him, drawing him even deeper. And all control left him. Her silky skin touching his, her warm breath upon his neck, her cold-hot hands strafing his scarred back.

Unable to stem the furious tide inside him, he began rocking into her. Slowly, achingly slowly, savoring each nuance of sensation, he felt her adjust to him, learn him and match his rhythm. When her fingers tightened on his shoulders, he withdrew only to plunge more swiftly into her, faster and faster still, driven by furious need.

Corrie felt as if he plundered her very soul. With every thrust, he seemed to awaken more and more of her. Her legs linked around his back, she could feel every pounding need he had. He filled her completely and still found more to discover. He began to murmur her name, almost as if in prayer. Then he spoke her name louder as he drove into her faster. Saying her name, driving deep. Calling her name, pounding against her. Faster and faster. And still it wasn't fast or hard enough. And she cried out his name, her hands on his jaw, her kisses drawing him closer and closer.

The fire he'd started in her suddenly exploded into a wild conflagration. She felt as if each part of her sparked and burst into flame. She clung to him, gasping his name, feeling the blaze of their passion washing over her.

Suddenly he stilled, deep within her, and called out her name once more, making it an imprecation, a desperate prayer, and she felt him shudder through her. She held on to him, despite being spun halfway across the universe. Involuntarily, she convulsed around him, more fully united with him than at any moment in her life. *Ah, at last. At very long last.*

On the heels of that sated thought, she heard a discordant note deep within her. Fire burns.

She clung to him as he seemed to turn to stone. And cried out when he called her name and lost herself in his release, in her own. It seemed hours before he gave a final shudder and uttered a groan, apparently trying valiantly not to crush her with his waning strength. He brought his lips to her collarbone and kissed her gently, seemingly reverently.

''Sweet, sweet Corrie,'' he said.

She couldn't answer, could only let her fingers talk for her. She traced the still, hard cords at the base of his neck, the rippled skin on his back and the sharp planes of his face. She convulsed around him as his lips nuzzled her bare breasts. He gave a low moan she echoed.

In all her years, Corrie had never known a moment more right than this one. And she never wanted it to end. And was afraid to ask what came afterward, the next month, the next day, even the next hour.

Mack felt Corrie's grip on him slacken and raised his head to see her eyes closing, a faint, utterly womanly smile on her parted and full lips. She was so beautiful, so irresistibly lovely. He longed for words to express everything she'd made him feel. But he couldn't find the perfect phrase, the best description, so in the end, allowed his soothing kisses to speak for him.

She murmured something and raised a languorous hand to his face.

Watching her, tracing the tiny smile on her lips, he wanted to promise her the moon, sun and stars all wrapped up into one pretty package. He wanted to tell her that he'd always be there for her. He ached to confide in her, to let her know about his past, his fears. And knew he couldn't do any of those things, though God knew she deserved everything he could possibly conjure up.

He knew more than most people that futures were uncertain things. That all one could truly hope for was doing one's best. And when that failed, the nightmares followed. He didn't want to drag her down into his haunted world. But God help him, he wasn't sure how he could walk away from her now.

"Mack...?"

"Mmm?" He smiled when she didn't open her eyes.

"This is the very best I have ever felt," she said simply.

He closed his own eyes against the sincerity in her voice, against her incredible gift. What could he possibly say to such bounty?

In the end he merely lowered his lips to hers and kissed her. Slowly, softly, and with all the promise he couldn't offer.

Chapter 9

As they drove through the ranch gates, Corrie felt as if she'd been gone for two months instead of a mere couple of hours. When she'd left the place, everything had seemed quiescent, sluggish, a dull rusty-brown with hints of green in the desert Southwest.

Now the seemingly sparse, newly formed plants in the garden beds flanking the veranda seemed to have burst into flower in the short time she'd been gone. Red and pink hollyhocks waved gently in the breeze, though their northern cousins wouldn't be blooming until late July. Beside them, an array of rich purple, yellow and white irises rose above their stiff leaves, making their common name of "flags" an obvious call. A spindly tree, a hybrid cross of a catalpa and a desert willow—*chitalpa*—had burst into an amazing array of white, orchidlike blossoms.

Corrie felt her hand clench Mack's arm. "Do you see that?" she asked.

He nodded, but she saw he was looking at the children in the center of the circular drive.

"Not them," she said. "That!" She pointed at the beauty beneath the veranda.

"What?" he asked, turning his eyes from the huddle of children and adults in the center lawn. He smiled at her. She caught her breath. Another miracle; Mack's smile no longer looked foreign on his face.

She dragged her gaze back to the flowers. "It was winter this morning," she said. She looked from him to the magical blossoms.

He chuckled. "And now it's summer?"

"No...*look*. Flowers."

He did as she ordered. His smile didn't fade in shock as she'd expected, seeing what she was seeing. Instead, he half chuckled and turned back to her in question.

She pointed. "The flowers. They weren't blooming yesterday. They weren't even blooming this morning."

He stared at the flowers as if stunned. "Oh, my sweet heaven."

"You see it?"

"Of course I do."

"It's a miracle."

He turned to her. His smile lit his blue eyes and turned them a deep blue denim color. The ice had melted. He reached a hand to her cheek. "You are such a sweetheart, Corrie. It's a miracle, all right, but a common one. This is the way it happens in the desert."

But, looking deep into his eyes, seeing so much more than he wanted her to see, Corrie was sure that

Rancho Milagro's magic was the real cause. The sun was shining brighter, the sky was bluer, and even the temperature had risen to a balmy seventy-five degrees in the couple of hours they had been absent from the headquarters of the ranch.

The blossoms flanking the veranda were a simple underscoring of the enchantment she'd found. The smile on his lips, his calling her a sweetheart, these were the real miracles.

She closed her eyes and opened them again swiftly. Mack still sat inches from her, and beyond him, the flowers still bloomed, a powerful combination of magic.

Corrie had been half-convinced both might disappear in the literal blink of an eye.

She was also afraid that every nuance of what she and Mack had shared at the ruined adobe dwelling would show on her face as happily as it did on the grounds of Milagro.

She needn't have worried. Everyone at the ranch was too busy worrying about what Juan Carlos had seen in the barn.

"Corrie, Mack!" Analissa cried out as they climbed out of the Bronco. "Juan Carlos sawed a ghost."

"It was La Dolorosa," Juan Carlos was insisting loudly from his place at the center of a human cluster. "She was all dressed in black and she walked right through Lulubelle's stall." He demonstrated this remarkable feat, looking more like a contortionist than a wraith.

Little Pedro shrank back against Jeannie's long skirt. "No. *Señora,* no. He's wrong. *No es verdad!*"

Analissa pulled on Mack's pant legs, and when he

looked down, she raised her arms imperiously. In a single sweep, he hefted her to his shoulder.

Corrie marveled that his features could be so impassive as the little girl wrapped her arms around his neck and squeezed tightly. He hid his heart from the children, she thought. But she saw his jaw work and the hand on the little girl's back splay protectively.

But he hadn't hidden a thing from her earlier.

Which one was the real Mack Dorsey?

"Was La Dolorosa all ugly and stuff?" Jason asked.

"Did she call your name?" Rita queried.

"She didn't say anything. And I don't know if she was ugly. She was old, I know that. About as old as Señora Leeza."

"Juan Carlos," Jeannie remonstrated as Corrie choked back a chuckle.

"Well, she was."

"I think you ate too many sausages at breakfast," Jorge suggested.

"That wouldn't make me see things. I eat lots of breakfast every day," Juan Carlos protested. "If you all don't believe me, why don't you go to the barn and look for yourselves!" It wasn't a question but a hot demand.

"Actually, though the way you said it was very rude, Juan Carlos, I think that's a pretty good idea," Chance said.

With a whoop, the children—with the exception of Pedro and Analissa—took off at a run for the barn. Almost as if on tethers, they slowed to a walk just before reaching the doors, then to a scuffling stop. Like marionettes, their arms dropped to their sides and all heads turned to look back at the adults.

Chance, holding up a hand to belatedly signal the children to wait for him, asked, "What did you two find out at the ruins? Any sign of our mysterious hitch-hiker?"

Corrie didn't dare look at Mack. "Just my duster," she said, cradling the coat of many pleasures to her chest. "No sign of the woman."

Something in her tone made Chance look at her a little more closely. "No sign whatsoever?"

She fought a blush. He couldn't know what had transpired between she and Mack. No one could.

"No sign at all," she said, glancing pointedly at Analissa to warn Chance that she didn't want to scare the little girl by revealing that they'd found no foot-prints. Of course, once Mack had kissed her, made love to her, there could have been a host of spirits and she'd never have noticed, let alone gone searching for traces of them.

"Curiouser and curiouser." Chance wriggled his eyebrows Groucho Marx-style as he quoted Alice on her journey through Wonderland. He gave a nod, which Corrie took to mean they would continue the discussion later, and looked questioningly at Mack.

"I'll join you," Mack told Chance. He looked at Corrie as if he might blurt out some deep truth, but only smiled instead. He shifted his gaze to the little girl in his arms. Their faces almost touched. "You want to stay with Corrie and Jeannie?"

Analissa shook her head, "No, you."

"How about you, Pedro?"

Pedro shrank deeper into Jeannie's skirt.

Mack nodded again before turning another inscru-table and level look on Corrie.

A thousand unspoken words fell into the unreadable chasm that stretched between them, Corrie thought. She lifted a hand, as if to touch him, but he'd turned away before she connected.

She watched the two men walking away, mentally comparing them—one boisterous and easygoing with a hard edge, the other quiet, somewhat forbidding, and fathomless. Even their strides underscored their differences. Chance walked as if he might have been raised at sea, a rolling, meet-the-ground gait. Mack walked almost like a mountain lion, cautious, wary and ready for danger.

But he was a lion carrying a little girl.

"Do you want a cup of coffee?" Jeannie asked.

"God, yes," Corrie said, but she was unable to take her eyes off the two men.

"I'll go put some on," Rita said, and all but ran for the hacienda.

"Such excitement," Jeannie said. Then, with a side-long glance she added, "I can see you and Mack are talking now."

Corrie didn't say anything as Jeannie reached down and took little Pedro's hand. "I don't believe in ghosts, do you?"

The little boy nodded.

Jeannie ran her free hand over his hair. "I think they'll find an old saddle blanket or one of Juan Carlos's jokes."

She led them toward the main house. "Feeling better?"

Corrie had to turn away to mask the smile that refused to stay hidden. She'd told Mack she'd never felt better in her life. She stared at the flowers blooming in the beds in front of the veranda—flowers blooming in the desert. "I'm fine," she said. "The flowers bloomed this morning."

"Isn't it amazing? And so gorgeous."

"Mack says it's common in the desert. For the flowers to suddenly bloom all at once."

Jeannie gave her another sideways glance. "So, you're not angry with him anymore?"

"No," Corrie said, but didn't elaborate. The fact that she didn't have to remained one of the things she most loved about Jeannie's friendship.

"Leeza missed all the fuss."

For a moment, remembering only how it felt to be in Mack's arms, struck by the flowers ablaze in their desert beds, Corrie thought Jeannie meant something else—it hadn't been a fuss, it had been sheer fireworks and more.

Jeannie continued, "She took off for the airport about a half an hour after you left this morning."

Corrie hadn't heard the ranch Jeep Cherokee pass the feeding track. She'd heard little but the beating of her own heart and the rich sound of Mack's passion-rasped voice. She wished she'd remembered to say goodbye to Leeza, however.

"How long is she going to be gone this time?" Corrie asked. She couldn't imagine ever wanting to go back to D.C.

Jeannie shrugged, stopping to turn her eyes back to the barn. "Who knows? She's thinking maybe a month or two. Maybe more. I guess it takes a while to do this last merger, though you'd think with all her practice, she'd be an old hand at it."

"The Land of Mañana is getting to her," Corrie

said, using New Mexico's local slogan instead of the state's official, "Land of Enchantment."

"Is it getting to you, Corrie?" Jeannie asked.

"Oh, yes," she said simply. The state—and Mack Dorsey—were changing her entire way of thinking. She turned her eyes to the barn, as well. The door to the cavernous interior stood open, but the shadows hid the group inside.

"I'm glad for that."

"We'll see," Corrie hedged.

"He's a good man."

"It's not a man who makes a place right," Corrie said stiffly.

"It sure doesn't hurt," Jeannie said.

No, it didn't hurt. In fact, except for a brief disappointment and embarrassment the night before, nothing about Mack Dorsey hurt. She felt wholly and gloriously alive.

And hungry.

And happy.

And suddenly, horribly frightened for the future.

Mack followed Chance into the barn, the little girl in his arms scarcely any weight at all. Her hands were linked behind his neck and her forehead pressed against his chin. He didn't like to think about the trust she was placing in him.

The other children, with Juan Carlos in the lead, pushed into the barn right behind them.

"She was over there," Juan Carlos said, pointing toward the farthest stall. "All dressed in black, like in the stories."

"You kids stay back, okay?" Chance asked, moving for the stall. "I want to see if I can see any foot-prints."

"The hay wouldn't show any. Ghosts don't have footprints, anyway," Juan Carlos said with the sure knowledge of the one who had seen the apparition. "But she was there. I don't need any proof."

"He still needs to look," Mack said, lowering a hand to Juan Carlos's shoulder. He kept his eyes on Chance.

The marshal had his back to the ghost hunters behind him and was squatting near the base of one of the horse's stalls. And Mack could tell by the way he sifted through the straw and straightened abruptly that he'd spied something that disturbed him.

"I know I saw La Dolorosa," Juan Carlos insisted.

"Did Corrie tell you we saw her last night, too?" Mack asked.

"No way! Tell me!"

"Corrie's back at the house. She's a better story-teller than I am," Mack said. "Why don't you guys all go there and ask her about it?"

The children hesitated for a moment, as if suspecting him of trying to get rid of them, then at his shrug, dashed for the main house. Analissa struggled in his arms and he set her down. She ran away from him like a caged animal released to follow her pack.

"Thanks," Chance said. "You saw?"

"That you found something, not what it was," Mack said.

Chance held out a strip of black cloth. Mack took it and nodded. "Wool. I'm pretty sure that's what our ghost was wearing last night."

"Doesn't prove much," Chance said.

"If it's not from someone's shirt or sweater, it pretty well tells us that whatever we've been seeing around here isn't a ghost," Mack said.

Chance frowned. "I'd hoped everything was over."

"You're thinking about the trouble you had last year?"

Chance shot him a sharp look. "That's about the size of it."

"From what I've read and heard about him, sending a ghost to do his work doesn't sound like your El Patron's style. He'd just send henchmen to kidnap the kids."

Some of the weight seemed to drop from Chance's shoulders. "You're right about that. He'd have sent flunkies in, guns blazing. Subtlety wasn't his strong suit. Luckily, most of his henchmen are in prison now."

"So who would send a supposed ghost?"

"That's the question, all right. You have any ideas?"

"Only one. What do we do about it?" When Chance didn't immediately come up with an answer, Mack added, "I understand you and Jeannie are heading out today."

"We can postpone that. It's just that Jeannie's first husband and daughter were killed in a car wreck three years ago this weekend. She has some notion of us going together to the graves. Introduce…hell, it sounds crazy."

"No," Mack said. "I get it. She wants to build a bridge. You, them, Dulce and José…the baby."

Chance looked at him squarely, a query on his face. "That's what she said."

"You have to go."

Chance nodded slowly. "But I don't like leaving the place when something's going on."

"We don't know something is going on. And even if there is, all we've encountered so far is a car-less woman with a torn shawl who's stolen a couple of burritos and a handful of cookies."

Chance gave him a crooked grin. "That sort of puts things in perspective, doesn't it?" He went back to the stall where he'd discovered the strip of cloth. He fingered a visible nail head. "No wonder she looked like a ghost. If her skirt or her shawl caught on this, it would have billowed out behind her, then, as it pulled free, it would have snapped out of sight—as if she vanished." He straightened and seemingly changed the subject. "Dulce tells me you've been training the kids."

Mack stiffened. He'd wondered when somebody might object. "A few basics. The buddy system, stuff like that."

Chance waved him to continue.

"You know, always keep an eye out for your buddy, and make sure he's safe, too. And how to defend yourself against a stranger if they grab you. Simple stuff."

"Don't knock it. It's a good idea."

Mack let out a pent-up breath. "Better to be prepared for things," he said, trying to relax again. He liked Chance and didn't relish going against the marshal's objectives for the kids.

"Be Prepared. You're just expanding on the Boy Scout motto," Chance said, and moved to the doorway of the barn. He gazed across at the main house. "Did

the kids you saved in that fire have your training?''
His voice was neutral.

''No,'' Mack said. He heard the screams, felt hot
flames licking at his face and hands. ''No, I hadn't
trained anyone.''

''Is the training a result of that fire?''

''I suppose it is,'' Mack said. *Help me...please,
somebody...help me...*

''If those kids had trained...?''

''I don't know if it would have made any difference.''

''I'd like to think it would have,'' Chance said, his
voice gruff with some unspoken emotion. ''I'd sure
like to believe that.''

''I would, too,'' Mack said. He felt as if the words
were torn from his soul. Maybe they were.

''In that house across the way are a group of children who need that training. They need every scrap
you can give them.''

Mack flinched as Chance's hand clasped his shoulder. The gesture was brotherly in a fashion. Man to
man.

He didn't tell Chance that there was also a woman
in there who made him want to feel whole again just
by smiling at him.

Chance said, ''You're right. We'll go. I feel I'm
leaving things in pretty strong hands.''

Mack wanted to protest that he'd lost five children
the last time someone had trusted him.

Help me...

He thought of the way Jeannie's hand ran over her
rising belly, the love she had in her eyes, on her freckled face, love for Chance, for the new baby, for the

future. He couldn't take this weekend away from them, no matter how little he might want the challenge.

Chance's hand squeezed on his shoulder as if driving in his message. "You can count on Pablo, he's a good man. I don't know much about Clovis yet, but he seems a stand-up sort of guy."

Mack felt the shifting of reins with Chance's every word and fought his instinctive acceptance of such a tremendous responsibility. He'd pulled ten children from a hellish inferno. He'd lost five. And he'd had to listen to their cries. *"Help me…somebody…help me!"*

Would the voices of his personal entourage of ghosts always call to him? Or were they some inner voice of his own, crying out against this onerous trust?

Mack almost sighed in relief when Chance's hand slipped from his shoulder. The marshal said, "You already have the kids in your corner. Seems your only problem is likely to be Corrie."

"Corrie?" Corrie of the chestnut hair and golden voice? Corrie of the desert sand, smile on her face, tears in her eyes?

"This training thing of yours, she's not going to like it much."

"What? Why not?" Mack asked, genuinely puzzled.

"She's a die-hard believer in the concept of kids being sheltered from bad things."

"Bad things happen," Mack said.

"Not in Corrie's world."

"Come on, she's been all over the known universe, reporting on every sort of atrocity."

"Exactly. I think she feels our kids here shouldn't be exposed to any of those influences."

Mack said nothing, trying to reconcile this other truth about Corrie Stratton.

"She's a dreamer, our Corrie. She's a lot like the fairy princess she looks, not wanting to believe in the big bad world. She wants them to live in fantasy land."

Mack took in Chance's statement but didn't believe it for a second. Chance was telling the truth as he saw it, but Mack was sure he didn't understand Corrie at all. She was a dreamer, all right, and she might look like an elfin princess, but she knew all about the big bad world. She knew it firsthand. And by knowing it, she wanted to provide the children at Milagro a magical place filled with wonder and awe; that didn't make her blind, it only made her vulnerable beyond reckoning.

"So you keep up with your training of the kids. They need it. Hell, I need it. We all do."

Mack nodded, feeling in some odd way that he was betraying Corrie.

"I'll drop off this piece of cloth at the lab on the way out of town this morning. I doubt they'll be able to find anything out about it, but, just in case," Chance said.

"As long as it's not made out of ectoplasm," Mack said.

Chapter 10

Corrie sat at her desk by the window. Tonight she made no pretense of writing lyrics. Her knees were drawn up to her chest and she rested her chin upon them, hugging them tightly with her arms. Her eyes, of course, were on the lit window across the courtyard and the figure pacing back and forth in silhouetted restlessness.

Dinner that evening had been a subdued affair. Once the discussion of La Dolorosa had run its course—repeatedly—Corrie had tried keeping up a thread of conversation. But without the lively Salazar foursome, Leeza's acid comments and with Pablo and Clovis both half-asleep at their plates, her attempts dwindled into mere ramblings.

She was grateful for Mack's suggestion for an after-dinner game and for the pleasantly cool evening and soft, lingering sunset that allowed the game to be played out of doors.

Mack assembled all the children in the circle of grass at the center of the drive. He had the children, Pedro and Analissa included, stand around him in a loose circle. They spun around three times with their eyes closed, then, when he called on them, they were to open their eyes and quickly close them again.

Corrie watched, baffled by the unusual game. When one by one, Mack called on them to describe exactly what they'd seen in that brief moment their eyes were open, she began to catch a glimmer of the game's meaning.

"The barn."

"Is the door open or closed?" Mack asked.

Watching from the veranda, Corrie had to look at the barn again herself to see that the door was standing wide open.

"Closed," Jason said.

Mack cupped his hands over his mouth and issued a loud raspberry, a game-show buzzer signaling error.

Jason giggled. "Open," he corrected.

"Good. Now, Juan Carlos, what did you see?"

"Two horses in the corral."

"What two horses?"

"Uh...Lulubelle and Dancer!"

Mack made the buzzing sound again.

"Lulubelle and Plugster?"

"Bingo," Mack said. "Very good. Any others?"

"No. Just those."

"Very good. And Pedro? What did you see?"

"My mother at the bunkhouse," he said in Spanish.

Corrie's eyes cut to the bunkhouse, an atavistic chill working up her spine. No one stood before or beside it.

Mack made the buzzer sound once again. "The bunkhouse is right. What else?"

"She's gone now," Pedro said, his eyes opening and closing.

Corrie's heart wrenched. They had only picked Pedro up twenty-four hours before. The boy had silently blended with the rest of the Milagro hoard and hadn't once asked about his missing parent.

Just before dinner, Corrie had called the authorities in Carlsbad, but no sign of Pedro's mother had turned up. The new sheriff had added a dark side to the little boy's story, however. "The mother's name is Lucinda Ortega. She's the live-in wife of a real loser, Joe Turnbull."

"What's a live-in wife?" Corrie had to ask.

"In the eyes of the law, they're not really married, as in filing a certificate somewhere, but Turnbull's her son's father and in her eyes, he's her husband. It's real common in these parts. California, too. Except New Mexico's not a common-law state, meaning poor Lucinda doesn't get diddly if she wants to divorce Joe."

"Tell me about this charming fellow," Corrie said.

"Charming, now there's a term I'll bet no one's ever labeled Joe Turnbull. He's got a rap sheet as long as my arm, and most of it made up of arrests for using Lucinda as a punching bag. She's tried getting away to family in Mexico, but he keeps dragging her back. His last arrest came after he assaulted the women's shelter she was hiding out in."

"What do you mean assaulted the shelter?" Corrie asked.

"Just that. He attacked the building with a baseball

bat and threw Molotov cocktails through the broken windows.''

''He could have killed someone,'' Corrie said, appalled.

''He did land a couple of women in the hospital, luckily minor wounds only. We got him out of there pretty quick, but the damage was done.''

''He's still in prison, right?'' Corrie asked, knowing the answer would be in the negative. The sheriff wouldn't be telling her all this if it weren't pertinent.

''Afraid not. He copped a no-contest on the vandalism and pled out the reckless-endangerment charge, so he only pulled a year's hard time. You gotta remember, he was arraigned in the days when El Patron was still running the county. I just had word that Joe got out two days ago. Nobody's seen him, but with the kid's mother missing, I've got a real bad feeling.''

''You think he did something to her.''

''Sad to say it, but yes. Pretty obvious conclusion. And that means he's probably still around here somewhere.''

''Do you think he might come after Pedro?''

''Could be. But it probably won't be to hurt the kid. In all the arrests, he was never cited for hitting his son.''

''Chance and Jeannie are out of town,'' Corrie said. Her statement wasn't nearly as irrelevant as it may have sounded.

''That's too bad, but you should be fine, way out there. Tell you what, though, have Pablo and whoever else is there on the ranch keep their eyes open, okay? And call me, day or night, if you spot anything out of the ordinary.''

She'd promised to do so and suspected the game Mack played with the children was his reaction to the phone call, though when she'd told him about it, his only outward sign of worry showed in the tiny furrow between his brows and the way he rubbed at his fingertips.

He'd acted as remote as ever, but she'd nevertheless had the impression he was more in tune with the new sheriff than she'd been. It was as if he'd taken on Chance's role at Milagro, though without Chance's grand storytelling and easygoing smile.

Throughout the somewhat subdued evening meal, his eyes had often traveled to the windows and the shadows outside. Corrie had wondered if he wasn't mentally walking the perimeter he so often patrolled at night.

Rita had joined her on the veranda for the second go-round of Mack's strange game. She watched for a few minutes, then said, "He's a smart man, Señor Mack."

Corrie nodded.

"He walks with his own ghosts, though."

"You think so?" Corrie asked.

"*Sí,* but they aren't like La Dolorosa. His ghosts only *he* can see."

"That sounds so sad, Rita."

"It is, *señora.* Very, very sad."

"I wish…" Corrie began, only to trail off.

"You wish you could help him, no? I wish you could, too. But it's hard to help someone stop listening to their ghosts when you have so many of your own."

Corrie turned to look at Rita. The diminutive woman, scarcely an inch shorter than she was herself, wasn't looking at her. Her eyes were combing the grounds outside the bunkhouse.

"It's a good thing he's doing," Rita said.

"What's that?" Corrie asked. "Teaching the children to pay attention?"

"Teaching them how to do it for their safety."

"They're safe enough here."

Rita's eyes cut from the bunkhouse and met Corrie's squarely. "Señor Mack knows. There's no safety anywhere for these children. For anyone. He knows."

Corrie wanted to argue with the housekeeper, wanted to tell her that these precious few lost children had been found, and they would have safe and happy homes at Rancho Milagro. But before she could summon the right words, the tiny woman did the oddest thing; she patted Corrie's cheeks and said, *"Pobrecita, niña,"* and left the veranda.

As she'd done when her friend Leeza kissed her forehead a few nights earlier, Corrie lifted her hands to the exact spots of the unusual caress and, inanely, still felt the warmth of Rita's fingers against her skin. What had the strange gesture meant? And why did the familiarity in her touch, and by calling her "my poor little girl" make her want to cry?

Mack set the children to patrolling the fences, checking the gates and inspecting the barns. He stood in the circle of grass, a man standing alone, watching the boisterous group of children run at the gates, the fences and the various outbuildings. As if aware he was being watched, he turned and met Corrie's gaze.

He lifted a scarred hand. It wasn't much of a lover's gesture, but it seemed to lodge directly in her heart.

She dragged one hand free from her cheek and held it out.

He smiled at her.

That was all he did. He just smiled. And her bones turned to liquid. It was like the sun coming out after a month's lengthy gloom.

"Interesting game," she called, though it was the least important thing she wanted to say to him.

He walked toward her, his catlike walk slow and deliberate, and every step making her insides quiver. Walking away from her toward the barn, he'd seemed wary, on the alert. Toward her, he looked dangerous, as if he were about to pounce.

"One you play all the time," he said.

"Me? What are you talking about?"

He looked up at her from the steps to the veranda. "You. You don't miss a single thing. It's in your nature."

She shrugged. "That's just training," she said.

"Exactly," he said. He mounted the steps.

Her heart was pounding so loudly, she couldn't have heard him if he'd spoken. In the distance, the kids were running from fence post to corral gate, checking each strand of wire, making a potentially deadly business a game.

"They're too young," she said faintly.

"They're having fun," he countered.

"There's no danger here," she said. "This is Rancho Milagro."

"A pretty name doesn't change reality. Danger exists, Corrie."

Her heart seemed to flutter at his use of her name. But she said, "It doesn't have to be here."

"It doesn't have to exist anywhere, but the truth is that it does. Life is cruel, it's not fair, and it's especially rough on the innocent."

"I don't want them frightened. Teaching them to see things in a dark light can make them afraid." She'd been afraid all her life. Every waking moment. And she'd chosen a profession where all she saw was more darkness.

Mack gave a wave at the children. "Look at them, they're having a ball. And they're paying attention to every little detail. How does that frighten them?"

She couldn't think. "It frightens me," she said.

He lifted a hand to her hair.

She jumped, but her eyes shifted to his. As always, she couldn't read his expression.

He asked, "Remember when you were a kid and the bell would suddenly go off signaling a fire drill?"

She nodded, unconsciously leaning into the warmth of his hand.

"Remember how teachers would have us line up quietly and make an orderly exit to the hall, then march single file to whatever door we were supposed to use?"

Corrie nodded again.

"But there was never a fire, was there?"

"No."

"No. And no one was panicked, no one was screaming, and no one was thinking for themselves, worried about their friends, remembering the way out if something happened to their teacher. No one even looked behind them, right? Because we weren't supposed to look, weren't supposed to worry, weren't supposed to even think. Right?"

Corrie nodded because it was all she could do. In his words, in his question, she could see glimpses of what had happened to Mack. Skin grafts because of burns, a fire, children screaming, utter pandemonium, a fallen teacher. Himself? She knew this, knew what had happened to him. She hadn't covered the story herself, no, she'd been out of the country, but she knew...something. But what was it exactly?

"What if, in addition to the fire drills, the system had added a few extras, like watching out for the people in front of you, beside you and in back of you? What if the kids had to keep their eyes peeled for the source of the danger? What if they were allowed to do a little thinking for themselves?"

Corrie only understood one thing clearly: however Mack Dorsey came by his scars, they were earned not just at a physically painful level, but at the expense of a huge chunk of his very soul.

Her breath burned in her lungs.

His hands grasped her shoulders, as if he might shake the truth of his statements into her, but he only caressed her arms and looked deeply into her eyes. "Quietly exiting a burning building doesn't cut it."

"But—"

"No buts," he interrupted. "Everyone should be *running* for the exits. They should *hit* the doors with all the force they can, *slam* through them, and with their arms around their buddies. They should fly through those doors and drop and roll. I mean really drop and really roll. Fire drills shouldn't be an exercise in who has the quietest classroom, but in pure, hard survival."

"You were burned in a school fire," Corrie said.

She wished she hadn't spoken the moment the words came out of her mouth, but she couldn't retract them. Not physically, anyway.

"Yes," he said. The answer was short, the emotion behind it, immense.

"I haven't asked where or how you came by your scars," she said.

Whatever fury had driven him just seconds before, drained out of him as he gazed at her. "You haven't. You're incredible."

"I'm not a reporter anymore, Mack. I'm not out for a story."

"I know that. I don't know what you are, exactly, but I know *that.*"

Tears unexpectedly welled in Corrie's eyes. "I don't know what you are either, Mack. I just know I care."

He tensed, ran a hand through his hair as if frustrated, but the look on his face spelled nothing but sorrow. "God, Corrie, I know that. And I care, too. Can't you see that? Can't you tell that it's driving me crazy?"

"Tell me about the fire," she said, not daring to touch him.

He turned back to her with the swiftness of a pouncing predator grabbing both her arms, scaring her a little. "There's nothing to tell, Corrie. I'm alive and they're dead. Okay? That's all there is to it. No heroics, just burned children and grieving parents."

She must have made some sound, for his gaze seemed to focus in on her—instead of whatever anger drove him—and he lowered his eyes to his hands on her upper arms. He emitted a low groan and released her, almost shoving her away before turning around to leave her.

"Mack," she called, unconsciously raising her hands to the spots where he had gripped her so fiercely.

He didn't stop.

"Mack, wait!"

If anything, he strode faster.

"Mack, I don't care what happened!"

At that, he slowed, stopped, then turned around.

"You should care, Corrie. Everyone on this planet should care. We train our children to be quiescent. We train them to follow the rules, obey the teacher, and above all else, to believe that they will be rescued. We don't tell them that if they don't think for themselves, fight and claw their way out of a bad situation, that they could die, they could just die. And we don't tell them that if they do, someone like me, someone who tried to save them, is going to feel guilty and scarred for the rest of his damned life. So scarred he can't even reach out to the most wonderful woman he's ever even imagined. So care, Corrie, but don't cry, because there's nothing here to cry about."

And with that, Mack turned and walked slowly, almost regally to the teacher's quarters. And every step he took seemed to echo in her soul.

Watching the pacing figure hidden behind the thin curtains over a lit window across a graveled drive, Corrie remembered Mack's answer to Jeannie's question the first night he'd sat around the Milagro table. In essence, he'd said he liked the prehistoric period because survival mattered.

Survival. Warmth, food, a mate. Leeza had teased him about being macho. He'd said something about matriarchal tribes, but the need being the same. Warmth, food, a mate. *Safety. That's all that matters,* he'd said that first night. That's what he believed with every fiber of his being.

A knock at her door made her nearly leap from her chair.

"Señora?"

"Rita," she said. Then on a sharper note, "Is anything wrong?"

The bedroom door opened. "Not to worry," Rita said, stepping inside Corrie's suite. "I hope you don't mind. I saw your light, no?"

"Nothing's wrong?"

"Oh, no. But you see, I'm here with the children, yes? And you watch Señor Mack's window, yes? So, why don't you want to go out there?"

"No. God, no. Let him be."

"Why?"

"What?"

"Why let him be? He needs something, *niñita.* And I think you know what that something is."

"I can't leave the children," Corrie said.

"Sure you can, *niña.* I'm here. Pablo's here."

Corrie couldn't hide the blush that rose to her cheeks at the suggestion. But she shook her head.

"He means something to you, that man," Rita said.

Corrie looked at the window across the drive. Mack's shadow crossed it. "Something," she said.

"Something very important, I think," Rita said.

"He wants to train the children. Like miniature commandos," Corrie said.

Rita sighed. "And there is something wrong in that?"

"They're just kids."

"They were only children where he came from."

Corrie turned to stare at Rita. "You know about his past?"

"Of course."

"Tell me."

Rita looked surprised. "I thought you knew. The newspapers and television called it the Enchanted Hills firebombing incident...."

Corrie didn't need any more than that single reference. Everything fell into place. Hero teacher rescues ten children. Five perish in firebomb set by disgruntled former employee. Of course she knew the incident, she just hadn't connected the dots. Ghosts, plural. Burns. The fire-drill analogy. The terrible, terrible scars. Five perished. The sleeplessness.

Rita had continued talking, and concluded with, "...so he's a true hero. And I think you should listen to his ideas. In the old days, when I was a girl, my father kept us all safe. He seemed hard by today's rules, maybe, I don't know. But I know that there are some things we have forgotten that we knew back in those days. Some of the simpler things to keep our families safe, to make our friends and neighbors as important as our own. Nothing so wrong with that."

"No, nothing wrong with that," Corrie repeated.

"So, you go out there to him. He needs you."

"I don't know what to say to him," Corrie said, but she wanted to go.

Rita held up her hands as if giving up on her. "So

don't talk. Have a little courage, *niña*. Life doesn't come in pretty paper packages. It comes with scars, and pain, and sometimes it's out in a little house just across a driveway.''

Chapter 11

Mack realized he'd been waiting for Corrie the moment he heard her footfall on the bunkhouse steps. He opened the door before her knock and didn't say anything.

"Mack?" she asked, as if he'd changed his personality since morning, had transformed into someone else. Maybe he had.

"Come in," he said, holding out a hand to her.

She stared at his outstretched palm for a moment, and her eyelids flickered when her fingers lightly slipped into his clasp. When she didn't come forward, he studied her more closely and saw immediately that she *knew,* that either she'd remembered or someone had told her about his past.

Her hand didn't flutter in his, as he'd half expected. It rested quiescently, perhaps trustingly, no attempt at escape.

"I've known Jeannie and Leeza since college," she said, her liquid brown eyes meeting his with a strange urgency. "But I've never told them this. Never even hinted at it."

He stilled himself, an unfamiliar combination of triumph and fear coursing through him. Triumph that she was sharing a secret with him, fear because such a sharing implied deep trust.

"When I was five, I got up in the middle of the night. The living room was filled with a cloud. A big pretty white cloud right inside our house. Usually the floor was cold, but that night, it was so warm that I lay down on it, watching the cloud floating over me. I heard a banging. Then I heard my mother screaming for my father and my father yelling."

He never wanted to stop someone more than he did right then. He would have given anything on earth to have Corrie simply break off her story.

"I'm not sure I realized right then what the cloud was, but I was scared and knew something was terribly wrong. Then I saw the flames beneath my parents' door. They looked like some kind of strange animal, jumping up from the crack under the door, leaping for the doorknob. I heard my mother call my name."

"Ah, God, Corrie, stop…"

"I was too scared to answer her. I couldn't move. I stayed where I was on that warm floor. My mother was screaming. My father, too. Screaming for me. And I couldn't move. Because I was too scared to move, my parents died."

Tears filled her eyes but she made no effort to wipe them away. Some fierce message seemed to shimmer in them, a meaning she desperately wanted him to understand.

"Corrie, you were a baby. Analissa's age. You couldn't be expected to rescue your parents."

"No? You couldn't be expected to run back into a burning building and sacrifice yourself for a group of children."

"I was an adult. Anyone would have done the same."

"No. No one else did anything remotely similar. I remember the accounts well." She gave a little moue. "Now, anyway. Maybe some part of me knew from the first minute I saw you. I tend to avoid stories about fires. Go figure. The point is, not one of the other so-called adults went back into that inferno. Not even the firemen went in. Just you." She lifted a hand to his face, not tracing his scars, but erasing them somehow with her touch.

"It's not at all the same, Corrie."

"Yes, it is. Because you're haunted by those you couldn't save, every bit as much as I am."

He wanted to argue with her, to deny it with every bit of bone and sinew in his body, but he couldn't because she was right and she knew it. *When Corrie Stratton says it's true, it's a fact.*

"I didn't come out here to make you feel bad or force you to think about that terrible afternoon. I came because it was time to let my secret be free, but only because I thought it might help you be free of your ghosts."

A slow river of tears coursed down her cheeks. "Because you're right, I was just a little kid and couldn't have saved my parents. And because you're wrong, you couldn't have done more to save those children.'' Her breath hitched and she caught her lower lip on a sob. She closed her eyes, but it didn't stem the silent tears.

When she opened them again, they were awash with sparkling tears. It killed him.

''And…and I came out here because you're right. The children do need training. If I had had any coaching, even enough to know the difference between clouds in the sky and smoke in the living room, then my mother wouldn't have died worrying about me, terrified that I was trapped, too.''

He didn't let her say any more. He dragged her into his arms, crushing her to his chest, breaking off her what-ifs, willing her to let his body absorb her pain, her misplaced guilt. He rocked her in the doorway, cradling her, murmuring her name, and trying so hard not to see that smoke-filled living room and the little girl who cowered on a too warm floor.

He didn't know when his comforting shifted. All he knew was that one minute he was fighting tears of his own, tears for a younger Corrie, for a frightened little girl who had to listen to the screams of her own parents, and the next, her hands were inside his shirt, skimming along his ribs and tracing the contours of his waist.

He didn't have the feeling she was trying to forget anything, but was driven by the same fierce need that seized him, a force beyond reckoning. Hers weren't the caresses of a woman attempting to lose herself in a single moment. Rather, they were the actions of a creature caught in the sheer, rough magic of living.

He dragged her into his living room and kicked the

door shut behind them before crushing her lips beneath his own. A fierce, possessive joy infused him. She was his and claiming him for her own.

She pulled at his shirt and he at hers. She pushed his shirt from his shoulders, dragging it down his arms. He slid her bra straps from her shoulders and unfastened the contraption with a groan.

He had to bite back an oath as she pressed her bare chest against his own naked torso. He'd wanted to absorb her pain with his body; he hadn't anticipated the sharp stab of agony he would experience when he felt her heart beating against his, knowing he would always want her like this, would always ache for her, no matter how wrong it would be for her.

When he'd kissed her that night behind the barn, then again later, lying on her duster, insensate with longing, with need, he'd half convinced himself that she was the reward for two long years of physical agony, the rainbow at the end of a terrible storm. But holding her now, having dried her tears with his own skin, feeling her breath against his collarbone, her heart thundering as if trying to join his, he knew a jagged despair, knowing the future wasn't a certain thing, that even the concept of a future was a huge leap of faith, the kind of faith he'd abandoned.

He longed for words to express what he was thinking, feeling, but couldn't find the very phrases he knew he should be offering her. All he could do was to let her understand some of his thoughts through his touch, and, through hers, his passion.

He dug at her jeans even as she yanked open his fly. He tugged hers down her silky thighs and she stood over him, her hands on his shoulders, her head flung back, her long hair swaying as if in a tempest.

"You are so incredibly beautiful," he said, a supplicant at her feet. A warrior kneeling before his lady.

Without rising, he ran his hands back up her legs, memorizing her, kissing her knees, her thighs, and hooking a finger on either side of her lacy panties, pulled them down to reveal her dark thatch of curls. He ran his hand over them, loving the springiness, the silken folds and honeyed moisture he found beneath.

Her fingers tangled in his hair and she gasped his name as his lips found another of her secrets and his tongue plied it free. He could feel her legs trembling and steadied her as he lifted one of them over his shoulder, granting him full access to her.

"Please…" she cried, her hands fisted in his hair, her stunned body aflame with need, with a raging thirst, and nearly inchoate in her desire. "Please…stop," she finally gasped.

He stopped immediately, holding her swaying form tightly against him. "Are you okay?" he ground out against her firm waist.

"No. Yes, of course, but I don't want to be alone in this."

He gave a rough chuckle. "I'm definitely with you here."

She blushed. "Not just with me. In me. Filling me. Please, Mack."

If she'd asked him to walk over burning coals, he would have.

In a fluid motion, he swung her leg from his shoulder and over his arm. He scooped up the other and surged to his feet. The look in her half-closed eyes made him feel godlike, powerful, endowed with super-human strength, though in truth, she couldn't have weighed more than a hundred and ten pounds fully clothed and dripping wet.

"I wanted to provide you a moonlit bed," he said.

"I'd like that," she answered demurely, though the look on her face was anything but prim.

He carried her reverently and somewhat arrogantly into his bedroom.

Though she knew the room intimately, having helped Jeannie decorate it, the well-appointed bedroom seemed a foreign place with Mack's possessions in it. A stack of books, an open magazine, a wall covered with notes and rough maps of the Rancho Milagro headquarters, and a queen-size bed with the covers turned back—all seemed to tell the story of the man who held her so securely in his arms.

She sighed as he gently deposited her on the bed. Her breath caught as he bent over her and lightly skimmed her lips with his. It felt like a first kiss, tentative and questing—as different from his intense passion as winter from summer. She found the contrast all the more alluring because it was barely controlled. She responded in kind, scarcely letting her fingers touch the skin on his back, on his shoulders.

He shifted lower, trailing featherlight kisses down her arms, across her breasts, an explorer with all the time in the universe. His teasing tongue discovered secret crevices and his fingers, hidden recesses and valleys.

He gently scooped her breasts into his hands, molding them softly, as if she were made of spun glass. His tongue flicked over a hardened nipple, causing her to draw in her breath sharply. His hands kneaded with more firmness as his teeth lightly grazed a hard nub. He suckled avidly as she arched beneath him, her fingers digging into his shoulders.

And he abruptly ceased his ministrations only to shift to her other breast, repeating his soft caresses, followed by intimate demand. He dallied and exhorted, he scarcely touched, only to follow the skimming delicacy with sure command. He kissed, nipped and kneaded every inch of her flesh, inciting a riot within her.

Mack moaned when Corrie touched him in return, groaned when her teeth gently grazed his tiny nipples, and swore when her hands reached between his legs, encircling him with her velvet hands.

She called his name as she thrashed in his arms. And he called hers, buried deep within her, losing every particle of himself and finding himself again afterward in the tears in her eyes and her languid smile.

When Corrie fell asleep in his arms, he was certain he'd never felt anything so exquisitely right in his entire life. That piercing sorrow washed over him again. He wasn't vain; the scars on his body wouldn't make her turn away from him eventually. She would someday run from the scars on his soul, the puckered wounds that would haunt him forever.

One day, some day, he would let her down. He would hurt her, or worse, fail to protect her. And on that day, at that moment, he would not be merely broken, he would be lost forever.

He reached for her hand when he heard a soft sigh, and thought it came from Corrie as she slept. Then, as he recognized her deep, steady breathing, he blamed the wind. Or someone crying far away.

His eyes snapped open and he turned his head. He hadn't been dreaming. Corrie still lay beside him. Her head was turned from his, a naked arm flung above her head, a leg curled outside the comforter. She was the embodiment of abandoned, guilt-free sleep.

He could still hear the faint sighing that had wakened him. Someone crying or murmuring.

He carefully inched from the bed. Corrie didn't move. He dragged his gaze from her and slipped to the window. He lifted a corner of the thin sheers.

Like a movie set, the ranch headquarters were illuminated by a thousand stars and a waxing, heavy moon. Shadows stretched and crept across the drive as the spring breeze teased the newly planted trees into dancing. A light at the back of the main house didn't illuminate the area outside, but looked warm and inviting in the darkness.

And someone was walking along the southern end of the barn.

A woman in black.

The *same* woman in black.

"What is it?" Corrie asked softly from behind him.

He couldn't hide his start. Nor the lust he felt for her upon seeing her naked beside him. Instead of reaching for her, he started dragging on his clothes. "It's the woman," he said.

Corrie left the bedroom and came back in seconds, already half-dressed. "What woman?"

"The one on the road."

She stopped in the act of buttoning her blouse. "La Dolorosa?"

"She's no ghost. She's out there by the barn."

Corrie sat down on the bed as if her legs had given out. "You're not going out there, are you?"

"I've got to."

"We can call the sheriff. He'll be here in—"

"A half an hour at the earliest. It's thirty miles to Carlsbad."

"At least call Pablo. And Clovis."

"And the kids, too? Give me a break. I think I can handle one woman," he said.

She gave him a look. "You don't have to prove that to me. The jury's already in."

He couldn't hide his grin.

"I'm coming, too."

"You're staying here."

"With my knitting? I don't think so." She'd moved to the window and was peering out. "I see her," she whispered. Then in a louder voice said, "Oh, I don't like this. What makes you so sure she's not a ghost? She looks like a ghost, walks like one...."

"Remember that piece of cloth Chance found?"

"Oh, yeah. That." She sounded unconvinced. Mack knew exactly how she felt. His insides were still shaking from his first glimpse of the ghostly figure outside the barn.

He pulled open a drawer and withdrew a small handgun.

"You have a gun?" Corrie asked.

"Chance gave it to me before he left. It's only a .25 caliber, more of a noisemaker than a threat."

"It looks menacing enough," she said.

"Good."

"I never thought I'd say this, but I'm glad you have it."

He turned for the door, intending to disregard her wishes and leave her behind. She matched him step for step.

He signaled her to be quiet and carefully opened the door. "Watch the creak on the top step," he whispered, creeping along the wall of the bunkhouse, avoiding the steps altogether.

He stopped at the end of the bunkhouse and peered around the corner.

The woman was gone.

His eyes strafed the shadows, but he couldn't spot her anywhere. He held out his hand at Corrie to have her stay in place. He slid around the edge of the bunkhouse, facing the barn with his back against solid adobe.

"I don't see her," Corrie whispered from right beside him.

He sighed. Corrie might call herself a follower, but she followed right where golden-voiced angels should fear treading.

"She's probably in the barn," he murmured.

"Can we call Pablo now?"

He gave her a look. "Why don't you do just that?"

She shook her head and stuck her hand in his back pocket. When he didn't move, she gave a half smile and shrugged. He'd thought her a potent mix before. He found her much more than that now. She was utterly unlike anyone he'd ever known. Childlike, all business, a dreamer, a skillful negotiator, soft and strong. Playful and wistful simultaneously. All woman in his bed, wholly game for a ghost search after midnight. She wasn't merely potent, she was irresistible.

"After you." She gave a forward wave.

"Stay behind me," he whispered back.

"No problem whatsoever."

They crossed the drive, making far too much noise. Once he stumbled over a large rock lining the drive, and a second later, she ran into him when he paused to listen. He ground his teeth and vowed to make adult training part of the safety ritual at Milagro, starting with Corrie and himself the very next day.

Thankfully, Corrie did hang back when he slowly opened the big doors of the barn. He didn't fumble around in the dark; he immediately flipped up the switches for the overhead fluorescents.

He heard a horse whicker softly. And heard a soft, choked sob.

With his gun outstretched, he made his way deeper into the barn.

"Hello?" he called out, first in English, then in Spanish. "Who's there?"

Another sob.

A child's sob.

And coming from one of the stalls.

"It's Pedro," Corrie said, materializing beside him.

Mack didn't ask how she knew the crying belonged to the little boy they'd retrieved from town; she seemed to know the tiniest of details. He only had to remember how she'd known exactly what troubled him the most. And what gift to offer to make even his darkest feelings subside.

"Pedro?" she called. "It's okay, little one. We're here. Where are you, honey?"

Another muffled sob led them to the boy. He was huddled in the back of an empty stall, half hidden by a pile of hay.

Corrie immediately knelt beside the boy. "I'm so sorry you're sad, Pedro," she said, her Spanish flawless, even if her voice was choked. "What can we do to help?"

"I want my mama," he sobbed.

"Of course you do, darling," Corrie said, sitting beside him and wrapping an arm around him.

"I want my mama."

Corrie drew him closer, pulling him onto her lap. She rocked him in her arms, her eyes meeting Mack's over the boy's head.

"I brought her some food," Pedro said. "I'm sorry I stole, *señor,* but I knew she was hungry. There was enough to share."

"Your mother?" Mack asked sharply, then softened his tone. "You brought your mother some food?"

"I saw her from my window. I climbed out to bring her food, but it wasn't my mama."

"I think we better get back to the main house," Mack said.

"Where is my mama?" Pedro sobbed.

"Don't worry, honey," Corrie said. "We'll find her."

"Why doesn't she come? Why is there a ghost?"

"There could be lots of reasons why your mother isn't here," Corrie said, feeling as if her heart were breaking. "But I'm sure she doesn't want you to be scared and sad for her. So let's go back to the main house and get you warm."

The little boy put his arms around Corrie's neck,

and she was grateful when Mack assisted her to her feet. He kept his hand on her arm for a moment longer than necessary and she glanced at him in question.

"I'll walk you back," he said. "Then I'm going to have a look around the barn."

She nodded, glad he would be with them on the short journey across the drive. The night seemed infinitely darker now, and more ominous. The boy had seen someone, just as they had. Some *thing* that wasn't the mother he'd been aching to see.

A distraught Rita and half-dressed Pablo met them on the veranda.

"*Dios mio,*" Rita said. "What's happened?"

"Pedro went to the barn, hoping to find his mother. He was taking her some food."

"I think I understand now," Pablo said.

"*Señora,* I'm so sorry I didn't hear him leave."

"It's okay, Rita. I doubt anyone could have. He snuck out the window. But we'd better get him inside now."

"I'm going to go back to the barn," Mack said. "I left the lights on."

"I'll go with you," Pablo said.

Until that moment, Corrie had forgotten that Pablo used to work for the federal marshal's office, and that he was Chance's cousin. In the dim light on the veranda, he looked formidable.

The two men nodded, almost in unison, and left the womenfolk and children.

"Are you all right, *niño?*" Rita asked Pedro.

"La Dolorosa was there," he said.

"*Dios mio,*" Rita said.

"I was scared."

"Of course you were. You're smart to be scared."

"I was looking for my mother. I was taking her two of your tamales. She would like them."

"I'm sure she would. We'll make her a big batch in the morning. And you'll help me, won't you?"

"And some of your cookies, too?"

Rita exchanged a glance with Corrie over the boy's head. "Such cheek." But she kissed the boy's head. "If you promise not to climb out any more windows."

"I promise."

"Then okay." Rita held out her arms for the child and, taking him, cradled him gently against her chest. "*Pobrecito*. Poor, poor little boy."

"Who did the boy see—his mother or La Dolorosa?" Pablo asked Mack as they entered the barn.

"I suspect the two are one and the same," Mack said.

"That's what I was thinking, too," Pablo said.

Mack went directly to the stall where they'd found Pedro. He pulled back the hay and discovered a Milagro blanket and a paper sack filled with tamales, a couple of broken cookies and an apple. The boy had included one of the canned sodas in this midnight picnic lunch for his mother.

"What did the boy say?"

"He said he was bringing the food to his mother, but when he got here, there was only La Dolorosa. Then he asked why there has to be a ghost."

"Jeez. So what do we do?"

"Not much we can do. Stake her out, I guess. Keep our eyes peeled. Especially at night."

"The boy claimed to see her—his mother, at any

rate. During that game you were playing with the kids earlier tonight?'' Pablo shrugged at Mack's questioning look. ''Rita told me.''

''Right. He said he saw his mother by the bunkhouse. Then he said she was gone. It struck me odd at the time, but I figured, poor kid, he's seeing what he wants to. Dumb. I should have checked the bunkhouse then. She was probably hiding in my own place.''

''Maybe. But then again, maybe it's really La Dolorosa. The new sheriff thinks Turnbull killed Pedro's mother and has her body hidden somewhere.''

''That makes sense except for one big problem.''

''And what's that, Señor Mack?''

''I can't bring myself to believe in a tamale-eating ghost.''

Chapter 12

Corrie felt as if she'd misplaced her mind somewhere.

The sun was shining brightly, the day dawning cool with ninety-degree temperatures predicted by mid-afternoon. The children, with the exception of a slightly heavy-eyed Pedro, were boisterously gathered around Mack for a new game, a variation on his training theme. Rita polished the front hall Saltillo tiles. Pablo and Clovis were out on the prairie somewhere gathering calves.

Corrie should have been thinking of a thousand different things—the children at the ranch, her dream of writing music, the bit of cloth Chance and Mack had discovered in the barn—but she couldn't seem to think of anything but Mack Dorsey.

Mack, with his icy-blue eyes that turned to cobalt fire when he couldn't speak, or to a deep denim blue when he was relaxed and smiling. Mack, with his scarred face that looked old before his time and yet felt brand-new. She thought of the way his passion stirred her as none other had ever done before. And more than that, she cherished his kisses that left her craving more even as she feared allowing herself to fully succumb to believing in a future with him.

Her hands didn't tremble when she was with him. Why was that? They'd trembled constantly, as long as she could remember. They'd shaken at her high school graduation, they'd trembled at every interview she'd ever accomplished. But they didn't shake uncontrollably, some portent of terror, whenever Mack touched her.

Such a little thing, but it seemed a powerful omen. Did it mean she was comfortable with him as she was with no one else? Or was she looking for meanings where none were needed?

No. It meant something. Something huge. A big thing to be acknowledged, to be reckoned with.

And, discounting the miracle of not shaking, he made her body feel sensual, sexy, and some restless part of her transcended. Oddly, this new inner peace and unusual confidence seemed to reawaken the journalist inside her. For the first time in at least two years, she actually wanted to do research.

She wanted to know every detail about Mack, every nuance of what he thought, dreamed or had ever wanted. She wanted to know what he liked for breakfast, what his favorite color might prove to be, and how many times his heart had been bruised in his life. She wasn't curious; she was obsessed with knowing these things and an infinite array of complexities in addition.

"Corrie?" Analissa asked from the doorway to her suite.

"Yes, honey?"

"Why are you inside? Mack's out playing games. Wanna come?"

Corrie waved the little girl over; her arms open wide. Analissa ran and leaped into her lap.

They giggled together as Corrie caught her and rocked her in her arms.

"Are you sick?" Analissa asked.

"Not a bit," Corrie said.

"Why aren't you outside?"

"I was thinking."

"Were you thinking about Mack?"

Everything in Corrie stilled for a moment, even as she took in the fact that Analissa was the only child who didn't give Mack a formal title. To this little one, he was "Mack." To everyone else, he was Señor Mack. Just as she'd always been just Corrie, never more.

"I guess so," she temporized.

"Are you going to marry him?"

Corrie knew the question wasn't directly personal. Most children Analissa's age asked such embarrassing questions only to gauge relationships in general. Corrie had listened to enough theories in her time to know how to answer the girl. "What makes you think I should?"

"Because he loves you."

That wasn't the prescribed answer. She was in deep trouble.

"And you love him," Analissa said dreamily.

Instead of trying to reason with the tiny angel in her arms, she tickled the child instead. "Love him? What makes you think that? Love him?"

Analissa giggled wildly and flailed ineffectively. When she couldn't seem to get her breath, Corrie stopped and hugged her tightly to her chest.

"Like, like that," Analissa said, gasping for breath. "That's why you love him. He makes you feel like that."

"Like what?" Corrie asked, though in the little girl's words she knew the answer. *Just like that.*

"That's how you feel about Mack. Laughing and crying at the same time."

Corrie chuckled. "I've never heard love described quite that way," she said.

"But it's true," Analissa said. She wriggled in Corrie's arms and wrapped her arms around her neck. "I love you, Corrie."

The little girl with jet-black hair and eyes looked straight at her, her youth disappearing in her intensity.

"I love you, too, darling."

The tears in Corrie's eyes blurred her vision of Analissa sliding from her lap.

"It's a happy time," Analissa said. "You did right."

"What's that?" Corrie asked through a choked voice, but she asked it of an empty room for Analissa had bolted through the door.

Though the little girl couldn't have known about the night before, it was as if her words had zeroed in on Corrie's confession to Mack. She knew instinctively that she'd done the right thing in going out to him the night before, in revealing her past, in melting in his embrace.

But she didn't know anything else she'd done right lately.

"It doesn't change anything," she admitted aloud. "He likes me. Wow. Stop the presses. And I don't think anyone's waiting for a banner header that says I like him."

She covered her eyes with her hands. "I've got to stop this. I'm brainless. I'm idiotic. I'm acting like I'm in love."

She stilled, Analissa's statement ringing in her ears. *"And you love him."*

She hadn't answered the little girl, not knowing how. But here, in the privacy of her own room, could she at least answer her own question?

When Corrie Stratton says it's true, it's a fact.

Was she in love? What did that even mean?

Was it love when she couldn't think of anything but Mack? Did love mean she couldn't see straight unless he was in her line of vision?

Or did it mean she was simply and wholly succumbing to the lure of Rancho Milagro, that wanting something was halfway to achieving it. Hadn't she told little Pedro something like that?

And Mack? What did he feel?

Corrie didn't have the sense that her actions, her confession, had changed anything but his uncertain feelings for her. He wanted her, she knew that much. And he admired her as well. But, if she left passion—passion that left her gasping for air and craving more—out of the equation, she was afraid he would hold her every bit as much at arm's length as he did the children.

But did he really stand apart from them? He carried Analissa as if she'd always been in his arms. He flicked Pedro's cheek with one of his fingers. He ruffled Juan Carlos's hair. He touched them, the little ones, the children; he let them hang all over him. She'd seen him only that morning, sitting on the front steps of the veranda, head to head with little Jenny, and her heart had constricted when she heard the little girl who never talked giggling with him.

He patrolled the grounds, walked the fences, taught the children history and mathematics, snippets of poetry. And he trained them against danger.

He carried them, jostled with them, made them call out dates and times, and accepted them as they were. And every child, from Juan Carlos to little Analissa, would call out tidbits of history, timelines and facts as they marched around the drive. And they loved it. God, they really loved it.

He wasn't an easy man. He was kind with the children, almost unfailingly, but abrupt with adults. He was sweet with her, in his rough way. And his touch could make her crazy and sated all at the same time. What did that mean?

What, on heaven's earth, did all that really mean?

Not everyone could be expected to lose themselves in stories as she did. And what did he do that was so different than herself, than Jeannie, than Chance? She wasn't distant with the children, not at all, and they adored her. Mack was distant, in his fashion, but the kids adored him as well.

A question popped into her head. *Did she adore him?*

Of course not, she answered herself swiftly. Adoration inferred blindness, a determined refusal to focus on reality. She didn't *adore* Mack Dorsey. She only wanted…

She didn't know what she wanted from Mack Dorsey. Everything, maybe. Everything and more.

If only he could be granted some measure of peace for the five children that perished in that fire, then perhaps there could be some glimmer of hope for a future together.

Even the word *together* scared her, made her want to pack a bag and run away as far as she possibly could. No matter that some corner of her heart had always yearned for union, she'd never, as Jeannie had—now twice—explored the dream. But unlike her, Jeannie seemed born for melding with a mate.

Corrie had decided years before that she simply wasn't the marrying kind. No man seemed to be able to touch her heart and she certainly had never tried reaching into theirs.

Until now.

She'd decided long ago that she would serve as the playful aunt to Jeannie's brood.

So why was she stumbling over the idea of marriage now?

Mack Dorsey.

And until she knew exactly how he felt, she wasn't about to go out on any proverbial limbs announcing her half-baked intentions.

She suspected Mack feared failing, but only because he pushed himself so far beyond reasonable expectations that failure was possible, even probable. In her case, she'd spent a lifetime living within the limits, doing her job, but never stretching the parameters beyond easy reach.

Maybe it was time to try. Maybe she could exercise the skills she'd acquired all those years at PBS and turn them to good use. To Mack's use.

And maybe, for once, to her own ends.

She dug out a yellow pad, a couple of fine-point felt-tipped pens, and cleared the desk in her bedroom. As she slipped her song notebook into a drawer, she caught a line she'd penned several nights before. "He walks with ghosts…"

She penned the line in capital letters at the top of a blank sheet of paper and picked up the telephone and punched in the numbers she'd used daily for ten years. After a few pleasantries with her loyal sources, she launched into her request. "I need a list of all of the survivors of that incident, okay? Particularly those he rescued. I also need a list of the parents of the children who died. And the cafeteria worker, too. In fact, I need everything." She gave the ranch fax number and her e-mail address.

Please let this work, she prayed. And then, in a secondary prayer, she added, *Please let me understand it.*

She didn't dare consider what would happen if her research only made things worse.

Rita called Mack to the phone midway through the afternoon. She began dusting the mantel in the living room as he picked up the receiver.

"You Mack Dorsey? Pete Salazar, here. Chance's cousin—his daddy was married to my aunt? Hell of a job you did at that fire. You're all right. Anyway, Chance dropped by a piece of cloth a couple days ago and asked me to run an analysis on it. He told me to call you if I had any luck.''

"Right. Anything?"

"I'd sure be interested in knowing where Chance found this scrap," Pete said.

Mack frowned. "On the floor in the barn. A nail in one of the nearby stalls had a black thread on it. We assumed the piece of cloth had been ripped off a shawl or skirt. Or maybe even one of the kids' sweaters. Why, is there something?" He glanced at Rita. She was busy replacing a small, framed photograph of Jeannie, Leeza and Corrie back onto the hearth seat.

"That explains the bits of straw, then. Of course, it doesn't explain anything else. The deal is, I've got a gal in crime-scene forensics looking at it now. She's been flipping out all morning. She's an expert on textiles. I called her in when our guys couldn't figure it out."

"Did she find blood on that scrap or—"

"Naw, nothing like that, but weirder. Ready for this? The wool in that little bit of cloth is hand-woven by a master weaver. That's strange enough, but now we get to the really good part. My textiles expert says this cloth was what she'd called wool-dyed, meaning the black color was added to the wool before it was even spun into yarn. And that the yarn was then coated with flax oil. That's linseed oil to us nowadays. Except this wasn't linseed, not in the modern sense.''

Though Mack was relatively sure Rita couldn't possibly be hearing what Pete Salazar was saying on the phone, her features seemed to pinch nevertheless. She whisked out of the living room and down the hall.

"Are you with me, so far? Not even a remotely current process went into the making of the piece of cloth."

Mack felt the hairs on the base of his neck tingling. "So because it was wool-dyed and has this flax oil on it, you're thinking this cloth is old?"

"You could certainly call it that," Pete said. "Linda says this little scrap of cloth is at least two hundred years old. Maybe more."

Mack's mouth felt dry, his tongue thick. He remembered reaching across the woman in black to open the back door of the Bronco. He thought of Corrie's duster, left behind for them to find. He pictured little Pedro creeping across the drive to present a midnight snack to his mama, only to find La Dolorosa, seeking her missing children.

"Could your Linda tell what the piece of cloth came from? Skirt, shawl, jacket, whatever?"

Corrie came into the room, Rita hard on her heels. Mack shook his head but raised his shoulders.

Pete said, "No way to tell. But Linda went on about carbon dating, DNA and other technical stuff. She says the wool comes from a type of sheep known only in New Mexico, Mexico and—are you sitting down? Afghanistan. Some kind of an angora goat, something the natives call Navajo sheep. She's as excited as I've ever seen her, and trust me, she's not that easy to rile up. She's already signed her name on the initial report, though. Bottom line is that swatch of material came from some bigger piece that's at least two hundred years old."

"I see," Mack said. He didn't see at all. Whoever had been in the Bronco that night they'd brought Pablo home had been real, not any revenant. And whoever—whatever—Pedro, Corrie and he had seen the night before was as real as the walls surrounding them, or the telephone receiver in his hand.

"There's nothing else, really," Pete said. "Couple of bits of hay, a few grains of adobe mud—also old, by the way, since it had evidence of very old manure in it. Kinda gross, if you ask me. Anyway, Mack, tell Chance all this for me and let me know if you find any more scraps of cloth like this. Linda's drooling."

Mack hung up the phone feeling dazed, but still sure the woman they'd seen the night before was every bit as real as the woman staring at him.

"That was about the cloth, wasn't it?" Corrie asked.

She had a smudge of ink across her forehead and a pen tucked over her ear. Her long, thick hair spilled out of its single pencil confine. As was common indoors, she was barefoot, her toenail polish rubbed off in places and bright in others. Her clothing was a rumpled collection of mismatched items that appeared to have been discovered at the bottom of a Salvation Army heap.

He didn't think he'd ever seen anyone as staggeringly beautiful in his life.

He felt something hard melting inside him. He couldn't help but smile at her.

At his smile, something in her eyes seemed to flicker. She smiled back, her harried features softening, a glow suffusing her face.

"The cloth?" she reminded him.

"That was Pete Salazar, Chance's cousin. He said there was nothing much unusual about the cloth—"

"Except?"

"Except that it was woven about two hundred years ago."

To his delight, Corrie grinned. "Really?"

Rita crossed herself and kissed the cross she'd taken to wearing around her neck.

"Two hundred years old?" Corrie asked, her eyes wide. She looked like a kid on the verge of hearing a ghost story.

"Yeah. Something about it being wool-dyed and some rare kind of flax oil."

"My grandmother used to spin her own wool," Rita said slowly. She crossed herself again. "She had a spinning wheel, and after we would shear the sheep, she would comb the wool and wash it, then comb it again. Then she would feed it into the wheel. I remember the sound of her foot on the floor, tapping a rhythm as her hand would send the wheel spinning and her fingers worked the thread."

"Did she use flax?" Corrie asked.

"She did something to it. Boiled something, mashed it, maybe. It stank, I remember that. She would have us hold the wands, which she wrapped with the twine, and she would dip her fingers into flax and rewind the yarn into balls."

"So the process isn't that unusual," Mack said.

Rita raised her eyebrows. "My grandmother was in her nineties when I was only ten. I've never heard of anyone doing it that way anymore. And people thought she was crazy then, when you could go to the notions store and buy yarn in any color."

"Hippies," Corrie said.

"What?"

"Back-to-nature types. You know, Foxfire groups, back-to-nature types, hippies. I'll bet they still do it."

"He was pretty adamant about it being at least two hundred years old, mentioned carbon dating and DNA testing."

"Dios mio," Rita said.

"What?" Corrie asked.

"She really is La Dolorosa."

The front door banged open, startling all of them, and Juan Carlos rushed into the room, panting, his hair flying, his eyes wider than they had been on a runaway horse. "She's here. La Dolorosa! We have her trapped in the barn!"

Chapter 13

The Milagro children and mixed-breed pups were gathered outside the barn, forming a rough semicircle in front of the great doors. Jason, Jenny and Tony huddled on one side; the little ones, Analissa and Pedro, on the other. Pedro was in tears and Analissa, totally ignoring her station at the barn door, was bent over slightly, trying to see his face and cajole him into a smile. The pups were barking excitedly, straining at their tethers.

Mack passed Juan Carlos at a dead run. "Stay outside, kids," he yelled before plunging into the dark opening of the barn.

Rita plucked at Corrie's blouse to keep her from following suit, but Corrie shook free, almost as easily as she passed the children in the yard.

The darkness of the barn was disorienting after the dazzling light of the drive. Corrie could barely see

Mack's shadowy form some twenty feet in front of her. But she'd made a study of his walk, his shoulders, and could have picked him out in a crowd of five hundred at midnight.

"Is she here?" Corrie asked.

"Quiet," Mack said.

She could tell by the way he cocked his head he was listening to something. He moved toward one of the farthest stalls. Corrie closed the distance between them.

A slight figure cowered in the corner of the stall, a black shadow.

Mack barked, *"Quien es?"* Who is it?

"Por favor, señor," a frightened woman's voice begged. "No dogs."

Corrie's heart melted at the note of fear in the woman's tone. She brushed past Mack and into the stall. For a moment, with her body between Mack's and the woman-ghost in the stall, she had the strong feeling she'd just crossed some invisible barrier between sympathy and stupidity.

"I'm sorry," the woman said in Spanish. "Please—"

This small, frightened woman couldn't begin to be dangerous. She didn't look nearly as ghostly huddled in the barn stall as she had on the dark ranch road that night. "It's okay," Corrie said, stepping closer. "You don't have to be frightened."

"I didn't mean to hurt anyone," the woman sobbed. "Please don't set the dogs on me."

"You didn't harm a thing, *señora*. It's all right. The dogs are outside. They wouldn't hurt you, anyway. They're only puppies." She took another step and held out a hand. Strangely, it didn't shake. "You're Pedro's mother, aren't you?"

"I'm so sorry," the woman said, and broke down into racking sobs.

Corrie could no more have walked away from the pain in the woman's voice than she could have turned her back on someone injured. She stepped forward and wrapped an arm around the thin shoulders of the sobbing woman. "Don't cry, *señora*. Everything will be okay."

"I didn't know what else to do."

"It's all right now."

"People were talking about this place of miracles. How happy the children were here. The police told me Joe was released from prison. I was scared, *señora*. He told me he would kill me the next time he saw me. I believe him. He's a terrible man, yes, but he doesn't lie. He will kill me. I had to get Pedro safe. Please, I had nowhere to go."

"Why didn't you just come with us that night on the road?"

Tear-drenched black eyes looked from Corrie to Mack and back again. "You only take children," she said with devastating simplicity.

"Oh," Corrie said, nonplussed. "But we wouldn't have turned you away."

Dark eyes, so like Pedro's, rose to meet hers. "No? I didn't know. I was only concerned with Pedro."

Mack cleared his throat. "So you abandoned him at the welfare office and then scared the others—and your own son—by pretending to be a ghost?" His voice was soft enough, but his tone and message rang sharp with censure.

She cowered against Corrie, beginning to cry again. Corrie threw Mack a hard look, angry he would be so callous.

He shook his head, his lips tight with barely checked anger.

"I didn't abandon him as you say, *señor*. I knew they would send him here. I hid on the side of the road when you went into town. You never saw me. I was going to be here when Pedro got here. But you saw me on your way back. You thought I was La Dolorosa."

"That doesn't make it right," Mack said.

"Mack," Corrie said softly. He couldn't know what desperate measures people might be driven to. She'd interviewed countless women in similar situations. At least Pedro's mother deserved a modicum of approbation for an innovative solution.

"As long as people just thought La Dolorosa was here, Pedro was safe enough. But if Joe hears about me, he will come. Promise me you won't tell anyone. I'll leave today. I swear it. But you can't let anyone know I was here. You have to watch over Pedro for me." Her voice hitched pathetically.

"And you," Corrie said.

"No! I can't stay here. I only came to make sure Pedro was all right. And to say goodbye. I bring danger."

"You're already here," Mack said gruffly. "And if your excuse for a husband comes around, he'll be asking for bigger trouble than he's prepared to face."

Looking at him, Corrie believed this. The ice was back in his eyes and he looked hard as proverbial nails and ready to tackle anything.

But Pedro's mother shook her head. "You don't know him, *señor*. It's like he has a demon in his soul. He won't care who he hurts to get at me. To take Pedro."

"At least he loves Pedro," Corrie said.

The woman looked at her as if Corrie had admitted she was a devil-worshipper. "He doesn't love Pedro. He believes he owns Pedro. That he can do anything he wants with him. And he wants to sell him like he does me. Or, how is it? Rent him out. Like a pimp."

Corrie's hands involuntarily tightened around the woman. "Over my dead body," she said.

"If Joe Turnbull has his way, *señora,* it will be. Believe me."

Corrie hid her shudder at the note of implacability in the very human voice. "Call me Corrie," she said, unable to think of anything to say as a capper to the woman's prediction of her own death.

Pedro's mother pointed at her chest. "Lucinda. Lucinda Ortega."

Corrie frowned, lost in last names. "Well, Lucinda," she said, leading the woman who was just a hint taller than she was from the stall, barely glancing at Mack's frustrated face, "let's take things one step at a time, okay? First off, I think it's time to let the kids see that you're not really a ghost. That reminds me. Are you missing a piece of your shawl or skirt?"

Lucinda shook her head, clearly baffled.

Corrie exchanged a glance with Mack.

"Never mind. Now, I think maybe Pedro would like to spend some time with his mama. Okay?"

Lucinda began to cry again. But these tears had nothing to do with sorrow or fear.

The children hung back as Corrie led Lucinda Ortega from the barn.

As always, Juan Carlos was the first to speak. "See, I told you she was real. Now do you believe me? La Dolorosa herself."

None of the other children ventured an opinion. They stared at the woman leaning on Corrie, their eyes wide with awe and an apprehensive curiosity—all except Pedro, who looked bolted to the ground. In quick succession, a series of clear expressions crossed his features: guilt, fear, worry and a pity for his mother that Corrie never wanted to see in such a young face again.

"Kids," Corrie said clearly, "this is Lucinda Ortega. She's Pedro's mother. She's going to be staying with us for a while."

Pedro's eyes shot to hers and held there. *"Verdad?"*

"Truly," Corrie answered with a smile.

The solemn little face broke into the most beautiful smile Corrie believed she had ever seen. "Mama!" he called, and sprang across the few feet separating them and straight into his mother's arms.

"Oh, Pedro. My big, strong son. I love you so much. You were so brave. So good."

"I was scared, Mama. Scared for you."

"I know, *jito*. I'm so sorry."

Corrie's eyes stung, snared by the tender reunion. When she glanced at Mack, she saw his jaw flexed as if he was swallowing emotions as well.

Analissa came to Mack and tugged on his pant leg before holding out her arms imperiously. With only the slightest hesitation, Mack hefted her to his shoulder and settled her comfortably on his side.

"Pedro's mama is a ghost," she confided. She patted Mack's cheek. "But we're not scared, right?"

"Not of her, pumpkin," Mack said.

"No, 'cause it's silly to be afeared of ghosts. Because they can be somebody's mama, right?"

Mack gave an involuntary chuckle and his eyes cut to Corrie's, sharing the humor before turning back to the child. "I never thought of it quite that way," he admitted. He smiled at the little girl and shared a slightly rueful grin with Corrie.

"No, because you're a growed-up."

Mack nodded. "I think all us growed-ups and the rest of you young uns ought to head back to the house for now, get Pedro's mama some food and let them talk for a while."

On the way back to the house, Jason took Jenny's hand in his. Corrie's heart wrenched at the shy smile the silent girl gave the boy.

She looked over at Mack. He'd witnessed the sweet moment as well. "It's easier for them," he told her softly.

"Easier?"

"Young love."

"I don't remember it being easy, exactly," she said. "But then, I don't think I was ever really in love."

"Never, Corrie?"

"Not—" She broke off. Not until now? Not really? Not like this?

He looked as if he'd say more.

Analissa patted his face. "Are you going to kiss Corrie?"

"Not here," Mack said.

"Why not?"

"Too hard to kiss somebody when I'm carrying somebody else," he said, and smiled at the little girl.

She giggled. "Me. I'm somebody. You love me, don't you?"

When he hesitated, Analissa snared his face between her tiny hands and pressed her forehead to his. "Tell me."

He gave a ragged chuckle. "Okay. I love you."

Analissa gave him a smack roughly on his eye. And firmly patted his cheeks. "I love you, too, Mack."

So simple, Corrie thought. The little girl had demanded Mack admit his love for her and he did so. Cornered, trapped by two sticky little hands and entreating eyes, he'd given her his heart for the asking.

She wished she had the courage to do the same. But knew he wouldn't feel the same compunction with her that he did with a vulnerable child.

"Now tell Corrie," Analissa said as she pushed his head sideways.

"Time to get inside," he said, his eyes briefly connecting with Corrie's.

Nice try, Analissa, Corrie thought sadly.

He swept up the steps and into the house without further pleas from Analissa impeding his swift getaway.

Corrie spent the remainder of the afternoon on the telephone, first with the sheriff, breaking Lucinda's confidence by letting him know the woman was alive and well at Rancho Milagro. She couldn't very well let him keep on searching for a dead body when the woman was presently in the kitchen eating tamales with her son. She told him what Lucinda had said about her husband, Joe, and the sheriff assured her he would keep her whereabouts under wraps.

"But, if I know Chance, he'd have my hide if you didn't get some help out there on the double. Trouble is, if I send a couple of deputies out there, Joe Turnbull would figure out the situation right off. He's dumb as a fence post about some things and smart as a fox about others. I think it would be better if we slipped in a couple of Chance's federal deputies. How about Ted? You know him, right?"

Corrie thought of the young deputy marshal so in love with Doreen from the post office, flirtatious single mother of three. "I couldn't take him away from Doreen."

"I don't think dynamite would do that," the sheriff chuckled. "But why not have Doreen and her brood out there for a visit, too? Nobody would think a thing of that. From what I hear, they go out there a lot, don't they?"

Corrie grinned. She liked the feisty postal worker and the kids would welcome her rowdy family. She realized with some shock that she hadn't seen what Leeza called "the horde" in only a scant week. It seemed months. A river of time since Mack had arrived there.

"I wouldn't want to put them in any danger," Corrie said. "In fact, I was considering taking the children out of here until all this blows over."

"With Ted out there, and the others—especially Mack Dorsey. You know Dorsey didn't say a word about who he was. Neither did Chance. I heard it from

Pete over at the crime lab. This Dorsey's the guy who rescued all those kids a couple years back in that fire.''

''Enchanted Hills,'' Corrie said. She felt a frisson of an unfamiliar emotion working across her shoulders. A bit of pride mixed with a strong dose of regret. Regret that she couldn't erase the losses from him, sorrow that she didn't know how to wave a magic wand and make it okay for him. Or for *them.*

''That's the one. He's a national hero. At any rate, with all that help, you're a lot safer right where you are than putting yourself at risk in unfamiliar territory,'' the sheriff said. ''In the meantime, I'm going to file an injunction against Joe Turnbull and have Judge Sanchez slap a restraining order on him. It won't do much—they seldom do—but at least we'll have some reason to arrest him if he gets anywhere near Lucinda.''

When she told Mack about the conversation later, he agreed with Eddy County's newest political appointment. ''And I'll step up the training with the kids. Have them keep their eyes peeled.''

''I don't want them scared,'' Corrie reminded him.

He took her hand. ''I thought we talked this out, Corrie.''

Her breath seemed to tangle in her throat as his thumb caressed her knuckles. ''It just seems that a focus on danger is unhealthy.''

''Tell that to Lucinda,'' he said. ''Or Pedro.''

''That's not fair,'' she said.

''Life's not fair, Corrie. Nothing about it is fair. Look at Shelley Vandersterre, Allen Parkins, George—''

''The five who perished in the Enchanted Hills firebombing incident,'' she interrupted, recognizing the names from her research.

"Trained caution far outweighs blind optimism,'' he said.

"I'm not advocating blind optimism,'' she said.

"No? Then what do you call it?''

"I call it not frightening children who have already been through enough in their lives.''

"That's specious logic, Corrie. How does teaching them how to watch for danger and giving them little ways they can help avoid it make them 'go through' something? Wouldn't danger springing on them unaware be so much worse?''

"Maybe. But I don't think that's what this is all about,'' she said.

"No? What is it, then?''

She struggled to hold in her thoughts, years of having done so trying to override the need to share her thoughts. "I'm afraid you're trying to undo what you feel is a failure two years ago. You couldn't save everyone then and you're beating yourself up for it.''

He looked at her for a long moment. "Wow. You know how to hit below the belt, don't you, sweetheart?''

Tears flooded her eyes. "Oh, Mack, I'm not trying to hit at you. I'm trying to tell you that you can't protect the whole world.''

"What does the whole world have to do with anything?'' he asked, but his face was pale, making the skin grafts all the more noticeable.

Everything inside her trembled, but she persisted. "You can't protect all of them all the time.''

"Hell, at this rate, I'll be lucky if I can protect any of you—them," he snapped.

She half flinched, and that inner voice that had told her to keep quiet issued a little I-told-you-so.

He glared at her, then to her amazement, he didn't walk away, strike out or even pound a fist against a wall. He sighed heavily and ran a hand through his hair. "Kids need to learn to provide some protection for themselves. Don't you see that, Corrie? If Shelley, George and the others hadn't panicked, hadn't felt trapped, they would have known how to get out. They were alive, Corrie. And because they didn't know any better, they're dead now. Burned alive."

The tears in Corrie's eyes spilled free. "Oh, Mack, I'm so—"

"Don't you say you're sorry, Corrie. I don't want you to be sorry. I want you to be mad. Be mad about what happened to you when you were a kid. Be furious, honey, that some bunch of pious jerks let you believe you were responsible for your parents' deaths. Hell, even be mad at your parents for not teaching you the difference between a smoke cloud and a rain cloud."

He did pace away from her then, stopped and looked up at the ceiling as if expecting an answer from above as he growled out, "God, when did we become such a passive society?" He whirled back to face her, his features fierce with the passion he felt. "We shouldn't accept devastating blows, we should rage and scream out against them. We should teach our children to fight and fight hard for their lives."

As she had thought before, she wondered if there wasn't a second message in his deeply felt words. She

wanted to reel away from him. To run. This man's
love was anything but passive. His love was ferocious,
albeit unspoken. She could see it in his face, feel it in
the energy emanating from him…had felt it in his
lovemaking.

If Mack Dorsey was offering her love, it wasn't
anything safe, it wasn't open and easy to understand.
It wouldn't be dancing on the surface of life. It would
be real, intense, vital and proactive.

"Don't you get it, Corrie? If we don't teach them
to fight, we're teaching them to be passive, to be vic-
tims. And I damn well refuse to be a party to that kind
of thinking. About the only thing we adults have in
our arsenal for them is the ability to help them learn
to be vigilant and teach them how."

Surprising her, he reached out and cupped her face
in his damaged hands that felt like silk against her
skin. "We can fight, Corrie. Us. You and me. We can
rail against acceptance. We can fight to get the drunks
off the streets so they can't kill husbands and babies
like that idiot did to Jeannie's first family. We can stop
the crazies before they enter a school with madness
on their minds. We can empower the weak to stand
up against the bullies of the world. These are the answers, Corrie."

Answers? They were prayers. They were million-
dollar treasure chests of hope.

"That's the real magic of this place."

She looked at him through a watery haze. "I don't
understand," she said.

"Face it, you fought a mountain of rules and paperwork to accomplish this. You've given up a career
most people would kill for in order to make a few

children's lives a little brighter. When I came here, I only wanted to escape the past, hide from the present. There wasn't a single thought of futures or happiness, or anything other than just getting by."

"What are you saying, Mack?"

"What I am I saying?" he asked back, as if truly questioning himself. "I'm saying, then I met you."

"Oh, Mack."

He lowered his lips to hers and kissed her with such tenderness that the tears that had sprung free earlier spilled over his fingers. He wiped them away gently.

"Don't you see what you've done, honey? You've reminded me that life is worth fighting for. You've made me believe that there is something that comes after the battle. Something that smells and tastes like a future. And I'm damned if I'm going to sit back and let some scudsbucket like Joe Turnbull, or some jerk like him, threaten it."

Corrie's heart was thundering in her breast. His anger had revealed more than she'd anticipated ever hearing him say. And so much that he didn't.

"You can't protect everyone, Mack. Not all the time. No one can."

"I have to try," he said. "And I'd like you to help me."

And this time, she nodded. Not because she was afraid to argue, and certainly not because she felt passive. She nodded because she believed.

Mack should have felt tense, teaching the children to sneak in and out of the barn. Instead, with Corrie beside him, turning the training session into a light-hearted game, he was almost as infected with hilarity as the children. Her throaty chuckle and her mimicry of various television bad guys had the children giggling, and even he was unable to hide his appreciative grin.

Strangely, her antics didn't detract from his objective one iota. They'd achieved an easy compromise without having taken the time to plot it out. She softened his hard lessons with kind words and laughter. And he punctuated her giggles with mock sternness, but always getting the point across.

Watching her, he was reminded of how they were together in bed. He the taker, she the giver, until the two blended and suddenly he was aware she was demanding all and he dying to give it to her. Soft meeting hard, fire melting in tenderness.

He'd been as astonished as she when he blurted out his feelings for her. Not that he'd given her all that much, but he'd given her more than he had anyone else in two long years. Perhaps more than anyone ever before. And it scared the hell out of him. He wanted to retract the words, to hide from the wistful blink of hope and realization he'd seen in her eyes.

And he wanted to tell her more. He wanted her to know just how wonderful he thought she was, that he could sit and listen to her for hours and hours, wallowing in her luxurious voice, or could lie awake all night just watching her sleep, her abandoned body sprawled akimbo, her breathing soft and steady. And what did all that mean?

That he loved her?

And why not? She was beautiful, kind and so incredibly expressive and responsive. Any man with half a brain and even a quarter of a heart would love her.

Loving her wasn't the problem. Believing he could be with her was the issue. Believing he could be a whole-enough man to provide for her, to protect her, to keep her safe and happy, that was the key. Wasn't it? To tell her he loved her would be simple. It would have the benefit of truth, but it would be without any sort of foundation for a solid future. He had too many ghosts, too many conflicts, too many doubts to drag her into that maelstrom of doubts.

And yet, watching her with the children, buying into his quickly improvised training, seeing her sneak around the barn, hearing her instructing the kids on the finer points of owl hoots, horse raspberries and toad calls, he knew he'd never wanted anything so much in his entire life as he wanted to believe in a future with Corrie Stratton.

Chapter 14

Where dinner the night before had been subdued, this evening's meal took on a party atmosphere, with little Pedro proudly presenting Rancho Milagro to his mother—who, as it turned out, spoke quite a bit of English—and with the other children enchanted with the notion of sharing a meal with a ghost, real or not.

Mack sat in his usual place between Corrie and Analissa, but, as Pablo and Clovis were still out rounding up the spring calves, and he was the only male adult present, his was the face the children looked toward for assurance, approbation or even a discouraging frown.

As Rita brought in dessert, Mack succumbed to combined pleas for a story and told the tale of Cabeza de Vaca's journey through New Mexico, making it an exciting, hair-raising adventure. Hanging on to his words every bit as much as the children, Corrie could see his gift for teaching inherent in each phrase.

And when he laughed and made some silly face over something Juan Carlos said, she suddenly caught a glimpse of the class clown.

Unaware that a smile played on her lips as she studied him, she was surprised when he looked her way and suddenly stilled, then slowly smiled back, his eyes warm, his gaze unwary, open. If ever a moment were more inappropriate to a declaration of her feelings, she thought, she hadn't known it. And yet, because he looked at her with such delight, such frank camaraderie, she wanted to blurt out the truth, whatever it was.

He'd said being there had made him want to fight for a future, believe in it. She wanted to let him know that he made her want to stand beside him for that fight. To be with him.

But how did one say that simply, knowing with a relative certainty that he would shut her out with an ice-blue stare, preferring the ghosts of his past to an uncertain future?

Lucinda insisted on clearing the dishes and disappeared into the kitchen as Rita and Mack led the children back outside for a quieter version of their afternoon recon training. Hearing the children giggling and the deeper rumble of Mack's laughter, Corrie felt she slipped a couple hundred notches deeper into a magical world, into one of the many miracles on this ranch. Just watching him smile made her want to laugh out loud. Listening to him laugh was enough to make her ache with a desire that transcended logic.

When the phone rang, Corrie barely started and picked up the receiver with a cheery hello. Her good humor slipped a bit when she heard the sheriff's voice.

To her mild irritation and rueful amusement, the man asked for Mack.

She called him inside and handed him the phone.

Mack gave her a wry look and deliberately talked directly to her. "Dorsey here."

She leaned against the wall watching him, blatantly eavesdropping. Even if the sheriff hadn't spoken so loudly, she would have been able to read the conversation from Mack's face.

"I've got some bad news," the sheriff said. "And it's my fault. Corrie Stratton told me Lucinda didn't want anyone to know she was out there, and it made sense. But, stupid cuss that I am, I didn't have the door closed when I was talking with her."

"And somebody was listening."

"Right the first time."

"And whoever was listening told somebody who ran into Joe Turnbull."

"That's about the size of it," the sheriff said. "Whenever you want to make a really crappy salary and get beat up on Saturday night by the town drunk, let me know and I'll make you deputy."

"Are you thinking Turnbull will come out here?"

"That's why I'm calling. According to my source, he's on his way right now, along with a couple of creepazoids that used to run with him."

"Oh, my God," Mack said.

Corrie merely tilted her head when he looked a hard question at her. She refused to give in to the fear that made her want to slide down the wall and huddle against the floor. She waved a hand at him as if making him continue.

The sheriff was saying, "I've already called Ted.

He and some of the deputies from the feds' office are on their way out there and I'm on my way, too. We should be there in about twenty minutes, give or take. But in the meantime, get the kids inside a safe zone and alert the others."

"I will," Mack promised. His eyes met hers.

She felt she might be as pale as writing paper and looking about as strong. Mack gave her a pained smile. He mouthed *It'll be okay.*

"Thank God you're there," the sheriff said.

Corrie frowned as Mack hung up the phone in a seeming daze. Then she understood. She didn't have to be a psychic to read his thoughts. They were written in the tabloids and between the lines of all the news accounts. If something went wrong, nobody would be thanking any deity that he was there. They'd be remembering the five children he'd lost in the Enchanted Hills incident. They'd compare the two tragedies. *So-called hero loses six more children in orphanage disaster. Hero or pariah?* And, even if they never blamed him, he would blame himself. And he might not be able to survive another such failure.

"It'll be fine," she said firmly. "They're right behind him. We just have to get everybody to safety."

He raised a haggard gaze to hers, and whatever he read in the depths of her eyes seemed to steady him. He squared his shoulders. "Right. Safety. That's all that matters."

She drew a deep, shuddering breath. She'd heard him say that before. It wasn't true, or even really possible, but right at that moment, she wanted him to believe it, to feel it. So she could have faith in it, too.

"I need you to be with me on this, Corrie," he said.

She held up a hand as if warding him off. "I know. No arguments. I'll get Rita and Lucinda and the kids—''

"The kids will be coming with me to the barn. And I'll take the pups. We'll arrange a few surprises for this guy. Just in case. Besides, it'll give the kids something to do. You get Rita and Lucinda—and yourself—into the bunkhouse.''

"Your bunkhouse? Why? You need my help with the children.''

"I want us separated. It's more difficult to go after people if they're in two separate locations. This guy's not going to think about you hiding in the bunkhouse. He's going to come straight for the house. The last time he went for Lucinda, I understand he attacked the shelter itself and waited for people to come running out. We don't want that to happen here. At least, I don't give a damn if he goes for the house, I just don't want him near any people. Houses can be rebuilt. People can't.''

"No. You're right," she said. "Bunkhouse it is." She thought of other options and swore softly. "Jorge went to town right after dinner. Should I call Pablo and Clovis on their cell phone?''

"Good idea, but I doubt they'd be able to get here in time to be of any help. It's still light enough for them to be riding, but in an hour or so, it'll be dark and that'd be dangerous.''

She nodded. She could breathe a little easier now and hoped a little color was creeping back into her cheeks.

He gave her an odd look, half speculation, half raw hunger. With a low growl, he leaned down and kissed her hard before pulling her to him for a swift, almost rough hug. She kissed him back equally fiercely.

"See you in a few," he said, releasing her.

She hoped that would be the truth.

Mack was already out the door, calling the children to a huddle, while she stood rooted by the telephone, aware that a pivotal moment had just slipped through her fingers.

In times of danger, a wise person admitted loving another. Did she love him? Did she truly love Mack Dorsey? How would she go about defining that, the way he made her feel? The way she suspected she made him feel? The lovemaking that left them both gasping for air and shuddering with passion?

The way her hands stopped their trembling when he touched her?

And this moment hung for a moment in the air. All she had to do was call him back and tell him how she felt.

But she stood there, watching him planning something with the children, not saying a single word about how he affected her, what she thought about him, what she wanted, needed and craved from him. She had, in fact, almost argued with him over such a minor point as hiding with the women in the bunkhouse where he'd made love to her.

And like so many moments, this exquisite one passed.

He glanced back at her and frowned. "What? Come on, Corrie, get a move on! This lunatic is on his way out here now!"

His words both spurred her into action. The children raced pell-mell toward the barn, followed by the lanky pups. Little Analissa tripped and cried out. Tony scooped her up without even slowing down.

The big doors closed behind them and Corrie realized the exodus had taken place so quickly she was still in the process of opening the kitchen door.

She'd been wrong to try stopping his training of them. She thought of Joe Turnbull on his way out to the ranch, how vulnerable they were. All of them. But thanks to Mack, they weren't quite as defenseless as they had been only a week before. They were still susceptible, could easily be wounded, and were probably scared, but they weren't without a few tricks up their little sleeves.

The one she suspected might be most vulnerable was the man ramrodding the operation. Because if anything happened to any of them, he would demand the hardest toll be taken on him.

She burst into the kitchen. "Rita, Lucinda? Quick. Your husband's on his way here."

"*Dios mio.*"

"Pedro? Where's Pedro?"

"Mack's got him. He has all the kids. He wants you to get to the bunkhouse." Unconsciously, she'd adopted the tone of command Mack injected into his voice. "He doesn't want Turnbull to find you and Pedro together. The bunkhouse is the safest place for you," she said. "Right now."

To her relief, the two women didn't argue with her. Rita automatically dried her hands on her apron and reached for Lucinda. "Come along, *niñita,*" she said. "Señor Mack will keep your son safe. He's a hero, you know. I'll tell you about it."

He was a hero, yes, but who would keep him safe?

No one had gone in after him in the Enchanted Hills incident. And he not only still carried the scars on the surface, but the unhealed wounds inside.

Corrie punched in Pablo's cell phone number as she watched the two women scurrying across the drive. She heaved a sigh of relief when she saw the door bang shut behind them.

Pablo answered on the fourth ring, cursing the hand-held device. Corrie didn't bother with preliminaries. She filled him in on the afternoon's events. "And now, Joe Turnbull is on his way out here and has a couple of friends with him."

"Did Mack call in reinforcements?"

She grimaced at his assumption that only Mack could handle things. Just as the sheriff had done. But she didn't belabor the point. Oddly, she would have made the assumption herself just a couple of weeks before. There was only one thing that had changed in her life, her meeting Mack Dorsey. Her innate faith in him.

To Pablo, she said, "The sheriff called Chance's office. Ted and a couple of others are on their way. And the sheriff."

"He's a good man even if he did steal my girlfriend in the fourth grade," Pablo said. "Okay, we're coming now. But we're about fifteen miles out, on horseback. It'll take us a while, even at a hard run." She heard him shout for Clovis to mount up. "Damn it. I had a bad feeling about going out yesterday."

"Is this Joe Turnbull really that bad?"

"Only if he's been drinking. Otherwise he's just a big, mean redneck. You hide the women and children, okay?"

Corrie grimaced again. "Mack's got the kids in the barn. Lucinda and Rita are in the bunkhouse. Mack said he's planning some surprise with the kids."

Pablo swore again, but this time with a chuckle. "I'll bet he does it, too. Trust him, Corrie. He's got what it takes."

"I do. I trust him with my life," she said.

"Good. You know he's crazy about you," Pablo said.

"I'd like to believe that," she said, then added, "because I'm so in love with him, it's a physical pain."

"Ah, then that's good, eh?"

Corrie found it ironic she could so readily admit her love for Mack to Pablo but never had come close to saying the words to Mack himself. She'd been so busy worrying about how he felt about her she'd forgotten to let him know that he might easily have a safe harbor with her. A place in which to be loved. A heart to live in.

She looked out the window as she ended the call with Pablo. The view reminded her of some of the magnetic puzzles Jeannie had purchased for the smaller children. The barn, the bunkhouse, the corrals, even the drive all looked exactly as they always did in the evening at Rancho Milagro: beautifully restored buildings the muddy color of earth glowing in waning sunlight. But all the people were missing.

Hiding.

This wasn't what she and the others had intended when they began the ranch, she thought. It was to have been a safe haven for the lost children of the world.

Almost as if connected to Mack's mind, she suddenly saw it through his eyes. The empty drive, the abandoned lawn, these were symbols that they were doing exactly what was intended, they were fighting for safety, banded together against a crazy man and his cohorts.

She saw the horses race away from the barn in the back corral, caught a glimpse of Juan Carlos herding them outside, before he disappeared back into the dark, hopefully safe interior.

She grabbed up one of the kids' baseball bats, the cell phone, and, of all things, Lucinda's shawl, and started for the front door, prepared to do as Mack ordered and join the women in the bunkhouse. She could hear the pups barking in the barn.

Glancing out the window, she saw a strange red-and-white pickup careening up the ranch road. Whoever was driving it managed the truck as if drunk, weaving back and forth across the road, sending a great cloud of dust behind him. Joe Turnbull was dangerous only if he'd been drinking.

"Dios mio…" she whispered, unconsciously adopting Rita's favorite phrase. Her breath caught in her throat and she inched back through the door, shutting and bolting it against the intruder.

Kneeling down and peering out the window, she saw with gratitude that Mack had already locked and chained the front gates.

But to her horror, the truck swerved into the field and, almost as if on two wheels, neatly circled around the gates. It smashed right through the wire fencing, tearing it out with a muffled groan of metal and wood ripped from the ground. The truck jerked to the left, then to the right, and shed the remnants of the fence.

And only paused for a split second before bearing straight for the veranda.

Though she knew it was impossible, she had the feeling the man driving the truck had seen her at the window and was coming straight at her. And although she felt adrenaline shoot through her, her primary, gut reaction was undiluted fury.

The idiot was going to drive right across the newly laid lawn, the lovely flowers and ram into the veranda.

She'd never felt real hatred before, but she recognized it now.

Mack didn't pause in his preparations for Turnbull when he heard the maniac plow through the fence. His heart lodged in his throat for a second when he heard the revved motor and knew the man was heading for the porch. A couple of well-placed rams on the right support poles and the whole portal could come crashing down.

Thank God, Corrie had taken the women to the bunkhouse. He'd seen them rushing through the door, a swirl of black skirts and flurried movement. It might be no safer in the long haul, but they only had to hold on until the sheriff and the U.S. deputies arrived. And that would be what, ten, fifteen minutes?

That was about all the time it took for five children to die in the Enchanted Hills disaster. A wave of despair rolled over him.

And, surprising him, following that wave came blessed, clean anger.

Those five weren't these six wonderful kids. The barn wasn't on fire. And if he had to die trying to stop him, the jerk in the pickup wouldn't touch one hair on these kids' heads.

Or Corrie's. Or Lucinda or Rita's.

He surveyed their handiwork. Even little Analissa was busy tugging on a bale of hay, getting nowhere with it, but busy nevertheless. Pedro leaped across the bale she struggled with and gave a mighty shove as the bale slid into place.

Behind the first zigzag line of hay bales were ball bearings, tacks and nails. Behind the second, puddles of molasses—a mess that had made Jenny wring her hands and worry about how they would clean it up. Behind the third row of hay bales, and stacked the highest, were most of the children, gloved and ready to throw sand in the men's faces before running as fast as they could out the back door.

Mack felt a sharp stab of panic. These were kids playing kids' games. A few bales of hay and some childish booby traps wouldn't slow down a man determined to get to his son.

"Now what, Señor Mack?" Juan Carlos asked.

"The bad men are running their truck into the house," Jenny shrieked from the front barn doors, her face pressed to the crack in the wood.

Slam!

"Turn on the water," Mack barked.

"Got it," Jason shouted.

"Good. Now, we've got to be very quiet from here on out. We'll just use hand signals, like this, okay?" He held up his hand. The children mouthed the words of the signals—stop, run, wait for it, get out of the barn. "And if the barn is on fire, what do you do?"

"Get outside, drop and roll," they all called out.

He motioned them to silence. ''Good. Okay, kids. Try keeping the pups quiet, too, okay? Now, this is the deal. We do nothing unless they try to come in the barn. Everybody ready?''

The children, varying in age from six to eleven years old, nodded with differing expressions on their young faces. Juan Carlos looked excited, though his face was paler than usual. Jenny looked almost angry, determined. Analissa clung to Tony's hand and appeared ready to cry. Jason's jaw jutted forward, his grip on the hose so tight Mack could see the boy's white knuckles. Pedro's eyes moved from child to child and, unexpectedly, he smiled.

Mack thought he understood. No one had ever fought for the poor kid before. The bogeyman that had plagued his whole life would have to face an army of Pedro's friends to get at the child this time. An army of kids and one resolute teacher.

Outside, the pickup's engine revved anew and gave an angry scream, before Mack heard another metal-wood impact and the unmistakable crack of a fired pistol. He realized the new sheriff was a master of understatement. The man in the truck was plain, old-fashioned nuts.

''Mack?'' Jenny whispered urgently, waving him over to the slit in the barn door. ''Look. Somebody's in the house.''

''What?''

She pointed. ''There. In the dining room window.''

Mack saw and his heart constricted painfully. *Corrie.* Sweet heaven, it was Corrie.

Another of the entryway windows shattered at the same moment he heard another crack of the pistol.

He had to draw the men from the house.

And he had to keep the men at the house, away from the children.

It was a devil's choice; either one causing harm. And doing nothing would surely drive him to do something that would result in some innocent's death.

Corrie's heart was beating so loudly she scarcely heard the pickup slamming into the portal supports. But she felt it. The impact sent a shudder through the house and she heard a window break somewhere.

She'd run into the dining room when the pickup first veered toward the house. From the relative safety of that room, she watched in horror as the big, blond madman behind the wheel actually laughed as he rammed the heavy round support pole holding the porch. His laugh made her feel insane herself. What kind of man would try to bring down the house he believed his son and wife were hiding in? And enjoy doing it.

As he threw the pickup into reverse, she half hoped he was finished, that some measure of rational thought had seeped into his brain, but when the engine gunned anew, spewing gravel out from behind the truck, she knew he would ram their beautiful home again. An icy chill worked through her veins, making her straighten. And she found the cold infusing her with renewed anger. It was a good kind of anger. A Mack kind of anger.

All her life she'd squelched any feelings of temper. She was so used to doing so, it was automatic. But she'd been angry with Mack a few nights earlier. She'd felt flickers of anger off and on for the past week. Those who had told her that anger was bad were wrong. Anger could be good, too. It could heal. And it could bring action.

Every injustice she'd encountered in her life seemed to coalesce into one focused rage at this small-minded little man who held human lives in such contempt.

Her eyes raked the rooms she could see, looking for some way to stop the man. Spying the alarm system switches on the wall, she raced across the dining room and threw the switch for the hacienda proper.

They'd never had to use it before, but the fire marshal had insisted it be installed when the building was first renovated. The shrill, pulsating screech nearly sent her to her knees.

To her delight, the alarm seemed to make the man behind the wheel of the pickup pause in his determination to drive right into the hacienda. If nothing else, the noise had made him hesitate, as if disoriented by the shrill racket.

And the fact that he hesitated gave her hope.

She smiled grimly and turned the alarm off.

The car motor gunned again.

She lifted the switch. It was an odd game of war with sound and fury. But she didn't feel a second impact. She flipped the switch down. Her ears still ringing, all she could hear was the whining hiccup of the man's damaged engine.

The sound of a car door opening wiped the smile from her face.

Mack winced at the strident scream of the fire alarm, sighed in relief when it cut off and swore softly when it came back on.

Jenny covered her ears. Then gave a little cry. "They're getting out of the car!"

"Get behind the hay," Mack ordered, and gave her hair a flick as she dashed to her station. He pressed his face against the barn door, trying to take in everything across the drive.

A man roughly the size of a large mountain had climbed out of the driver's side and his two—thankfully much smaller—friends were still struggling with the passenger's door. They finally broke free and staggered toward the front of the battered pickup.

"Lucinda!" the largest of the three men yelled at the house, his voice barely rising over the sound of the alarm. "You get out here, you bitch!"

The alarm ceased.

Stay down, Corrie, Mack willed. Stay down and *stay safe*.

One of the other men fired his pistol into the air. The third grabbed at his crotch. "Come outside, Lucinda. We got something for you."

The man with the gun giggled a high-pitched hyena's cackle.

Already tense, Mack stiffened even more. The men were dead drunk. Through the crack in the barn door, he could see them weaving toward the veranda steps. One of them tromped on the flowers Corrie had admired so much.

Mack's jaw tightened. He would keep the kids safe, he promised himself. And the others, too. But afterward, when all was said and done, he'd find a way to pay that one back for destroying Corrie's innocent pleasure in her seemingly miraculous flowers.

His hand jerked reflexively when the big one he

assumed was Joe Turnbull jumped up onto the veranda. The man had to use the support pole he'd tried destroying to maintain his balance.

"Lucinda! Get out here!"

"Time for that jerk to pass out," Mack whispered, and even as he did so, wondered if Corrie was whispering her little prayer, *I'm Corrie Stratton, and if I survived my childhood, I can survive this.* He knew why she said it now, knew the phrase had been born the night her parents had died.

He should never have left her in the house; he should have made certain she and the other women were out before he took the kids to the barn. Stay down, he silently commanded her.

The only rational thought in Corrie's mind was keeping the men outside long enough for the sheriff to arrive. No matter how many surprises Mack had in store for the madman, she didn't want them anywhere near the children—or Mack.

Something hurtled through the French panes of the dining room window, sending shards of glass across the lovely room. A rock thudded against and skidded across the dining table, scarring the wood. Leeza, who picked out the table, probably would have killed the man right where he stood.

She flipped back on the switch for the alarm. This time she didn't even flinch when the horrible racket ensued.

"Lucinda!" she heard a man yell over the screeching alarm. He punctuated his demand by furiously pounding on the heavy front doors.

Corrie reached up and cut the terrible alarm off.

The pounding abruptly ceased.

"Lucinda?"

Corrie wanted to yell at him to go away, that the police were on their way, but remembered what Mack had said about the man attacking the house first. Better to keep him occupied here than send him anywhere close to the children and Mack.

"I know you're in there, you bitch! Get your skinny butt out here and bring the kid with you. How the hell am I going to pay for that wool you like so much if you and the kid don't do your jobs? Huh? Tell me that, bitch!"

One of the other men laughed vilely. "Yeah. My cousin, he's waiting. He likes the little boys."

Corrie slammed the alarm back on, blocking out the filthy stream of abuse. If the sheriff didn't get here soon, she would find a gun somewhere and kill these bastards herself.

The blaring alarm sent the men outside reeling away from the door. She was grateful for the clamor as it drowned out the vile oaths she was sure they were yelling at her.

Get here soon, she commanded a distant Ted.

Then, to her horror, she saw the flicker of a lighter reflecting in the shards of glass on the dining room floor.

"You want to play games, bitch? Eat some of this!" A flaming wad of cloth sailed through a broken window and landed in the center of the Saltillo-tiled entryway.

Dark clouds of smoke choked up from the wad of material, and as the flames danced around it, she re-

alized one of the men had torn off his shirt to use as
fodder for a fire.

She stared at the blaze in the center of the floor and
felt the past merge abruptly with the present. Terror
swelled up in her. Fire, she mouthed as silently as she
had when she was a little girl. Fire.

She dragged the alarm switch down, cutting the
noise, throwing the house into sudden silence once
again.

"I'm not five anymore," she murmured. "And
you're going to pay for that little cloud."

Chapter 15

The children's pups, little more than a year old and more used to being petted than proving their mettle, and pushed beyond their ability to obey commands, had taken up a frenzied barking at the repeated use of the alarm. When the penetrating screech ceased abruptly, the four pups went into a delirium of howling protest.

In the silence, Mack was sure the sound was as equally cacophonous as the alarm itself. He swore when the largest of the three men whirled drunkenly and faced the barn.

"Lucinda! I'm going to get you. You think you can hide from me? No way!" the man yelled, and lumbered down the steps. His two friends—one of them naked to his scrawny waist—staggered behind him.

To his intense relief, Mack saw a shadow move behind the broken windows in the main house and, less than a second later, the flames he'd seen inside were doused. Corrie was all right. And thinking.

Safe? Please, let her be safe.

"Lucinda! You stupid bitch, get out here right now!"

"You might try a new line," Mack growled beneath his breath. He held up his hand to signal the children.

Something hit the barn door with an enormous thud.

"Lucinda!"

The alarm in the main house went off again. The three drunks approaching the barn whirled and faced the house. The one without his shirt lost his footing and fell heavily to the dirt.

With children and booby traps behind him and three drunken oafs in front of him, Mack thought that some dark-humored god somewhere was probably laughing. But laughter was the furthest thing from his mind. Despite the overt black humor, these three men with room-temperature intelligence quotients had spent the afternoon liquoring up enough courage to come attack a helpless woman and her six-year-old son.

They'd found enough bravery in a bottle to fire up somebody's pickup, drive thirty odd miles and try ramming it through a house that for all they really knew, contained only foster and orphaned children of assorted young ages. They'd drunk enough joy juice that they screamed threats of rape and destruction, and had literally torn the shirt off one of their backs to light the place on fire.

What was the difference between these silly and stupid men and the lunatic who had despairingly thrown a firebomb into a crowded school?

The answer was simple, Mack thought. *Nothing.*

The two weren't different at all. They were simultaneously ludicrous and dangerous. That was the saddest
and most damning comment about madmen he could
think of.

The buffoon who fell pushed to his feet and swayed
dizzily. The alarm stopped as suddenly as it kept turning back on. "Turnbull, I'm going to nail your wife
for that, man," he growled. "I hate that noise."

Joe Turnbull approached the barn with the caution
of a rabid dog, head down, eyes bleary, body poised
for a fight. His thick arms swung from his side like a
man aching to swing the first punch. "She ain't over
there, anyways. And I'm the only one who's gonna do
her tonight," he said. "*Lucinda!* Get your ass out
here!"

Mack, still with his arm upraised, backed away from
the barn doors.

"I mean it!"

Something heavy thudded against the barn door.

Analissa squeaked and the pups resumed their furious barking, their yelping holding new tones, a ferocious mixture of anger and fear.

"I wanna go now," Analissa cried out. "I don't
like this game anymore."

"It's not a game, Annie," Juan Carlos hissed. "You
gotta be quiet."

"Tell them to go away, Mack."

Mack threw her a look over his shoulder. His heart
wrenched at the sight of her tear-streaked face and big,
frightened eyes. He had to get these men away from
the barn, away from the children. As far away as possible, without sending them to either the main house
or where the other women were.

"I hear you in there!" Joe bellowed. "You send Lucinda out. And Pedro. We're not here for nobody else. You send them out or we're coming in." He punctuated his demand with a few well-placed rocks against the side of the barn.

"The sheriff's on his way," Mack shouted. "Get the hell out of here or you're going back to prison."

"Yeah, and who's gonna make me? Your big-shot marshal's done flown the coop. I seen him leave with his pretty little wife and their Tex-Mex kids yesterday."

Mack studied the rafters above him, the children beneath. All he had to do was get the kids out, shut all the doors and windows, and he could light the bale of hay on fire. Then the idiots outside would have something to be sorry about. He even pulled a pack of matches he'd tucked in his pocket earlier.

"Who's that I'm talking to, anyways? You're not Pablo, the little weasel. And you sure aren't Clovis. I know, you must be the new candy-assed teacher." He laughed derisively then said in a falsetto voice, "Oh, Ruiz, I'm so scared of the big bad teacher man. Save me."

Mack ground his teeth to withhold any response.

Something hit the doors again. This time they bent inward and the bar lock gave a suspicious groan.

"You're making a big mistake here," Mack yelled. "I've got a .38 and I'm sure as hell not afraid to use it on the likes of you." Where in blazes were the troops?

Someone fired a round through the barn door. Had Jenny still been standing at the crack, she'd have been

hit. As it was, the bullet passed through the pine plank-
ing not an inch from Mack's waist.

"There are children in here, you idiots," Mack
yelled. "Stop shooting and get away from the doors."

"You coming out?"

Mack glanced over his shoulder at the tense children. Every eye was on his still-raised hand. Slowly
he nodded and dropped his hand in a slashing motion.
Like puppets, they disappeared behind their curtains
of hay. It was like asking them to take cover behind
glass walls.

Even the pups seemed aware of something new
about to take place and their anxious yips fell silent.

"Fine," Mack shouted. "You back away from the
doors and we'll open them."

He heard one of them say, "It's a trick, man, don't
do it."

"Hell, it doesn't matter if it's a trick or not. They
got my kid. And he's mine. I do with him what I want.
No goddamned teacher's gonna take him away. If I
wanna kill him, that's my right. I brought him into this
world, didn't I? Shoot the damned door again, Ruiz."

"I don't know, Joe. Getting your kid's one thing.
Killing one, like that's a sin."

"Just shoot the damn lock off," Joe snapped.
"When did you get so worried about sin? Besides,
what do you care about other people's snotty-nosed
kids, huh?"

"I got a kid," Ruiz said.

"Come on, you pussy. Give me the damn gun and
I'll shoot the damn door down myself."

Mack looked back to make sure the kids were still
down behind their less-than-solid hay bales before

sliding into one of the empty stalls himself, one that afforded him a clear view of the doors and the children at the same time. As if his movement signaled Joe Turnbull, the drunken madman suddenly fired at the door.

While the door held, Mack was less grateful for that than for the satisfyingly dry click signifying an empty gun. Unfortunately, the men seemed undeterred by the lack of that weapon. They were drunk enough to feel invincible and mean enough to try anything.

One of them—probably Joe—charged the door. It bowed in with a shrill whine of protest.

"Help me, goddamn it," Joe hollered.

The door bowed again, and with the extra pressure, the bar snapped free, spinning off its hinges and slamming into the stall Mack hid behind.

The pups yelped and one of them gave a shrill howl. But it wasn't the noise or even the sight of only two men charging into the barn that had Mack's heart threatening to stop completely.

Little Analissa stood up from her hiding place and clearly yelled, "You're bad, bad men. You breaked our door."

Watching in sheer horror as the men separated, one running in a drunken parody of the spy routines they'd practiced only that afternoon, and the other two breaking through the barn door, Corrie flipped the alarm switch again. And shut it off immediately when only the smaller of the two in the doorway glanced over his shoulder at the main house.

One of the men, the big one she'd identified as Joe

Turnbull, gave a huge guffaw, and punched his friend hard enough that the man nearly fell.

Corrie knew that even in moments of extreme tragedy, humor existed, often bloomed, but she found the fact that these men laughed while terrorizing children to be the consummate abomination. There was nothing funny about two grown and obviously drunk men terrorizing children.

Chapter 16

Mack couldn't see what drew the men's attention but would have recognized Corrie's voice from a deep coma. "No," he growled. *Stay down.*

But he understood what she was doing. She'd seen the men break into the barn. She might even know what happened to the third jerk.

He heard a second voice call out, one he thought was Rita's.

Juan Carlos had pulled Analissa down and she was noisily crying in his arms. The pups were barking feverishly.

The missing third man screamed from behind the barn.

To his horror, Mack realized Jason, his man with the water hose, was missing.

The two men in the doorway of the barn had their backs to him. He picked up a two-by-four he'd set against the wall of the stall earlier. He silently slipped from behind the barrier and ran, pulling back the two-by-four as he moved, directly toward the big man's broad back.

He didn't know if the men heard him or had the drunken fool's luck of seeing the swing coming, but they both turned.

The two-by-four connected with Joe Turnbull's shoulder instead of his back and the man bellowed in rage and pain.

The smaller man ran for the barn's interior and he caught the back swing of a two-by-four wielded by a man who had been a fair tennis coach a couple of years before.

"Get him!" Mack heard Juan Carlos yell.

Not taking his eyes from the staggering Turnbull, hoping the ringing in his ears was really the sound of sirens in the distance, Mack could see that Turnbull's pain was secondary to his fury.

The big man turned and with a roar charged Mack.

From her position on the front veranda, Corrie saw Mack's well-placed hit on Joe Turnbull, then on the man without a shirt, and felt a fierce jolt of satisfaction course through her. She felt like jumping up and down, cheering Mack on.

She didn't know what had made the man behind the barn scream but when she looked in that direction, she wanted to scream herself. She saw a pillar of smoke rising from the back of the barn.

"Not a cloud," she whispered.

Then she saw the third man, the one who had

screamed. She saw him backing away from the barn. And she saw the gun in his hand.

Without conscious thought, she raised the baseball bat in her hands, much as Mack had done the two-by-four, and started forward. She gained momentum as she descended the steps. Suddenly, in the crystal clarity of action, she understood Mack, understood herself. She could no more have stood there and have done nothing than she could have buried her head in the sand.

She wasn't a coward; she never had been. She just hadn't known how to turn emotion into positive action. There was nothing more positive or proactive than to fight for people she loved.

Like a woman possessed, she launched from the veranda, determined to get to the man with the gun before he used it on Mack or one of the children.

The two-by-four in his hands was about as effective as a toothpick when the angry Joe Turnbull lumbered forward. He raised a huge fist and rammed it at Mack's face. Though he ducked, the fist still connected, driving him backward into what was left of the barn door. Through a haze of dust and pain, he saw Turnbull pivot around unsteadily, ready for a second attack.

Mack pushed to his feet and stood with the two-by-four in both hands, barring the man from the barn's interior. The mountain lunged at him.

Like a matador, at the last possible second, Mack sidestepped Joe Turnbull's attack and the big man's rage propelled him into the barn, into his friend and took them both over the first hurdle. They screamed as they landed on the ball bearings and tacks.

The children cheered; Pedro loudest of all.

Mack risked a glance at the bunkhouse. Rita stood on the steps, wearing one of his blankets as a shawl, all dressed up like a child on Halloween. She crossed herself and gave a little wave.

Corrie seemed to be flying across the drive, so swiftly she ran toward him. "I love you, Mack," she yelled as she veered to the left and disappeared around the corner of the barn. The baseball bat in her hands looked like an extension of her arm.

He felt as if she'd hit him with it. She loved him?

And told him so in the middle of a battle with three drunken thugs?

He laughed aloud. Somehow it was fitting. Right. Great, even. He felt infused with power, with strength, with a heady, giddy joy. He turned back to the men struggling to get up from the ball bearings and tacks. The children, instead of maintaining their posts, clambered up on top of the bales of hay and threw sand at the men.

Mack laughed anew as a mostly blinded Turnbull tried lunging at little Pedro and slipped on a ball bearing and landed heavily on the tacks a second time. Mack added to his general discomfort with a not-so-friendly whack of the two-by-four on his thick skull. The man groaned and slumped down, not fully unconscious, but nowhere close to being able to attack small children.

The pups barked happily, racing back and forth on the bales of hay.

And Mack heard a gunshot. It sounded like a .38, the same caliber he'd lied to the men about having. He ducked instinctively and whirled around. No one stood behind him and the men on the floor weren't armed.

"Fire!" Tony screamed from the back door of the barn. "Fire!"

A sickly pale Jason, sporting a gash on his forehead, limped into the barn and started spraying the back wall with the garden hose.

"Mack?" Tony called. "Jason's hurt."

"Is it bad, Jason?"

"I'm okay. But I think the man shot Corrie."

"What!"

"Corrie's shot."

Mack felt the blood draining from his face. Every instinct in him demanded that he run to her.

"The fire's all around her. She hit the man who hurt me. She hit him with a baseball bat!"

Mack couldn't breathe. Couldn't think. All he could envision was Corrie's blood pouring out into the dirt, her glorious body surrounded by fire. A little girl on a too-warm floor.

"Oh, God," he moaned.

"What do you want us to do?" Tony yelled.

A devil's choice, but the decision could only go one way. He couldn't leave the children. He had to secure them first.

With no more compunction than he'd have felt for swiping at a tail-raised scorpion, Mack swung his two-by-four and smacked Joe Turnbull friend's hand as he was reaching for Analissa. Mack grabbed the little girl and swung her out of the barn. "Run to the bunk-house," he yelled. He yanked Jenny from her perch and all but flung her out the door. "You, too, Jen. Run like the wind."

"Juan Carlos!" he barked. "Get out. Now!"

"But—"

"Now! And take Pedro with you."

The boy grabbed hold of Pedro's arm and propelled him off the bales of hay and out the barn door.

"Tony, you get the dogs. Hurry!"

Tony grabbed at the leashes and managed to round up the four dogs and stay out of reach of the two men in molasses and fence tacks. Mack gave the men a harsh reminder of who was boss as the boy dragged the dogs from the barn.

"The barn's on fire," Turnbull whined. "You can't keep us here."

"You pathetic excuse for a human," Mack growled. "You're the one who set the blaze. You were willing to kill little kids—" *and* Corrie? "—and for what? Power, control? Because you found some courage at the bottom of a keg? Let you up? I don't think so, you bastards. I hope you cook in your own juice."

"Mack?"

"Jason! Forget the water. Just drop the hose, okay?" Mack yelled. "You go out the back way. I don't care how far the fire's traveled." He looked up and could see flames licking along the roof. And he could see the boy was limping. "Can you walk?"

"I'm okay. He just knocked me down."

The boy ran as best he could, dragging his leg.

Mack quickly reviewed the children in his mind. Analissa and Jenny. Juan Carlos, Pedro, Tony and Jason. All were accounted for.

He gave Turnbull and his pal an extra two-by-four love tap. "And that's for Corrie's flowers."

He ran out of the barn and hesitated only long

enough to count heads on the bunkhouse steps before racing around the corner of the barn in search of the woman with the golden voice, liquid eyes and trembling hands made for holding his heart.

Strangely, despite the fire, Corrie looked as if she were sleeping in a ring of brightly colored streamers. As she had slept with him, one arm was flung above her head, one leg crooked and to the side.

Beyond her, away from the worst of the fire, one of the three thugs lay in a heap, a baseball bat some two feet beyond him and a gun within inches of his fingertips.

Mack turned, as though in slow motion, to see rescue racing down the ranch road, sirens blaring, lights flashing. They whipped around the still-locked gates, following the path Turnbull had carved.

He ignored them and, still trapped in that sense of the universe having slowed down to a crawl, made his way through the flames to Corrie. He lifted her and walked back through the flames. He felt the heat but it meant no more to him than a breath on his skin.

He never gave her assailant a thought as he carried Corrie out to the circle of grass in the center of the drive and laid her in the lush green. She didn't move. Didn't moan.

"Corrie," he said.

His hand was shaking so badly, he couldn't feel her pulse. He couldn't see the rise and fall of her breasts through his swiftly gathering tears. "No, Corrie. You can't go now."

"I love you," she'd called, running for a bad guy armed only with a baseball bat.

Around him men were yelling, dogs were barking,

deputies were shouting. The barn fire took on a roaring life of its own. For all it affected him, the chaos might have been taking place on another planet.

Mack knelt beside Corrie. Blood seeped from a wound just beneath her left collarbone. He yanked off his shirt and wadded it into a pad to staunch the flow. She didn't move.

He sank to the grass, sitting hard, unable to think, unable to feel.

"Is she alive?" the sheriff asked him.

Mack didn't answer. He pulled her limp body into his arms and cradled her against him, terrified to discover the answer to the sheriff's question. If he didn't know, he could still pretend, couldn't he? He could still picture a future, a life. But he couldn't do that if he knew that she was dead. He would never be able to see a future again. Because without Corrie, there was no meaning in a future. None at all.

He rocked her in his arms, unaware tears were running down his scarred cheeks, heedless of the mayhem around them, conscious only of his love for this rare and wonderful woman.

"Ah, Corrie. Wake up, Corrie. Don't leave me. Ah, please."

He felt little hands on his back, on his shoulders, and knew the children had gathered around them. "Kids, you shouldn't be out here."

"But the police have rounded up all the bad guys," Juan Carlos said, then asked, "Is Corrie dead?"

"She can't be dead," Analissa said hotly. "She's Corrie. She's going to be my new mama!"

"Is she okay, Mack?" Tony asked, his voice breaking.

He felt little sticky hands on his face, swiping at his tears, pushing him to look at Corrie. "Analissa, please," he said.

"Look. Her eyes are opening, Mack. She's not gonna be a ghost, are you, Corrie?"

"Corrie?" Mack asked, his voice raw.

"You love me, don't you?" she asked weakly.

Analissa forced his head into a nod. "He does, see?"

Mack gave a hitching chuckle.

"You love me, don't you?" Corrie demanded. "Tell me."

"I love you, Corrie."

"That's good, because I love you, too."

"You told me."

"I was afraid you hadn't heard me. You were busy at the time."

"I would never be too busy to hear you."

"I had to stop him, he had a gun," she said. Her eyes fluttered shut and fear clutched at his chest.

"Stay with me, now," he said.

"Is this a proposal?" she asked.

He felt a moment's stunned surprise. Then grinned at her. "Yes. Yes, it is. Will you marry me, Corrie Stratton?"

Her coffee liqueur eyes opened. A haze of tears filmed them, making them bright. "Yes, Mack Dorsey, I will marry you, because I love you with all my heart and never want to spend another day without you."

"Is that true?" he asked.

"You know it is," she sighed.

"Good, because you know what they say? 'When Corrie Stratton says it's true, it's a fact.'"

Chapter 17

Finally back at Rancho Milagro after a week in the hospital, Corrie still ached a little if she moved too fast, but the doctors in Carlsbad had assured her that she'd be right as rain in no time and that she'd been strangely lucky. If she hadn't rushed so close to the man with the gun, the bullet might have nicked her heart or pierced her throat. A couple of inches either way. As it was, it passed straight through her on a slightly upward angle, missing every major artery and organ.

"Are you sure you're up for all of them?" Jeannie asked.

"I'm positive," Corrie said firmly. "Where's Mack?"

"Giving them 'be calm' instructions. Think they'll listen?"

Corrie grinned. "He's the one who's been teaching them to think for themselves."

Jeannie's face paled and Corrie knew she was thinking of the narrow brush they'd all had only a week before.

"They did fine," Corrie said. "We all did."

"Yes, you did," Jeannie agreed, and brushed her hand across her eyes. "Why didn't you ever tell me about your parents?"

"It seems stupid now, but some part of me really did believe it was my fault."

"Like Mack," Jeannie said.

"Yes. Like Mack. That reminds me, would you get me that stack of papers on my desk? I have something for him. I'd almost forgotten it."

Jeannie was back in seconds and handed her the sheaf of papers, blatant curiosity on her freckled face. "What's all this?"

"They're interviews with the children Mack saved at Enchanted Hills. And their parents. And the parents of the ones who didn't survive."

"Oh, Corrie."

"Every single one of them thank Mack from the bottom of their hearts. Even the ones whose children perished." When she caught Jeannie's look of warm speculation, she didn't try to hide her blush. "I had lots of time in the hospital."

Rita interrupted them from the door. "Can we come in now, *señora?* They are going to have fits if they don't see Corrie pretty quick."

"Sure," Corrie said. "Let them come in."

Rita gave a signal and everyone from the ranch filed in. The children came first with Analissa in the lead, followed by Jenny, Pedro, Juan Carlos, Jason, Tony, José and Dulce. The ranch hands came next, Pablo,

Clovis and Jorge, all with their hats in their hands, looking so much like Dorothy's trio of friends from Oz that Corrie had to smile. Rita and Lucinda walked in together and were closely followed by Chance and Mack. Leeza came in last, a surprise visitor.

No one spoke.

"What did you tell them, Mack? That I would break if they said anything?"

Analissa gave a little shriek and leaped onto the sofa. "You're not a ghost!"

Corrie chuckled and gave the little girl a kiss.

"She will be if you keep bouncing like that," Juan Carlos said. He stepped forward and handed her a bouquet of wilted daffodils. "We saved these in the garden."

"They're lovely," Corrie said. "Thank you."

"You helped save our lives," Tony said. "And you got shot doing it."

"I saw the man shoot you," Jason said. "I went out there when he screamed and he hit me with his gun."

"Does anyone know why the man screamed?" Corrie asked.

Everyone exchanged glances.

"I'll settle for a guess," she said, smiling.

"He told the police he saw La Dolorosa behind the barn."

"But he screamed when I was still on the porch," Corrie objected.

"And so was I at the bunkhouse," Rita said. "Lucinda was with me."

Jason said, "But he says he saw La Dolorosa when he was lighting the fire. And she walked toward him.

He screamed. Then I sprayed him with the hose and he hit me. Then you hit him with the baseball bat and he shot you.''

"Dios mio," Rita said. "La Dolorosa saved us. It's a miracle.''

"And Mack saved Corrie. And now you have to marry him," Analissa said from her comfortable niche against Corrie's good shoulder.

Jeannie handed Mack the sheaf of papers Corrie had put together.

"What's this?" he asked.

"It's for you," Corrie said. "And a new start for me. I realized what I really hated about journalism was the distance. I want to write from the heart, from the inside of a story. I want the emotion.''

"About time," Leeza said. "And are you going to write about Rancho Milagro?''

"I'm probably too close to this one.''

"I would imagine Joe Turnbull would enjoy reading it in prison.''

"He can read?" Pablo asked.

"He'll never be bothering Lucinda again. He's up on eight counts of reckless endangerment, five vandalism charges, three attempted murder counts and a host of little charges, like reckless driving, driving while under the influence and others.''

"And his pals?" Clovis asked.

"They're going to be sitting behind bars for a long time, too.''

"Couldn't happen to a nicer couple of guys," Jorge said.

"And we're staying here, right?" Pedro asked.

"Yep," Mack answered. "Rita needs a hand with the messes you guys make all the time."

"Who's that?" Leeza asked from the newly repaired front window.

"Who?" Juan Carlos asked, dashing to the window to peer out.

"That woman walking away down the road."

"La Dolorosa," Juan Carlos whispered. Then, with excitement, "It's La Dolorosa!"

The Rancho Milagro crowd, including Corrie, gathered around the front windows. They fell silent, staring out at the lonely figure in black walking down the road, walking away from the ranch.

Rita said quietly, "The bad luck goes now." She crossed herself. *"Pobrecita."*

"Maybe she brought us good luck," Corrie said. "She may have saved our lives."

"And Rancho Milagro," Jeannie said.

Mack wrapped his arm around Corrie and kissed her temple and whispered, "And you. She brought me you."

"I like this place," Analissa said. "We have lots of ghosts."

"You saw her, everybody? I told you. I told you she was real," Juan Carlos said.

Chapter 18

The sun had set in a spectacular splash of red. The children had gone to their beds sated after a homecoming feast that outdid all Rita's previous lavish meals. Jeannie and Leeza had fussed over Corrie until she couldn't stand it anymore and had come looking for Mack.

She felt as if she'd been searching for him all her life. *Seek and ye shall find.* She rapped on his door. *Knock and it shall be opened unto you.*

Mack stood in the doorway, his eyes warm with welcome, his hands reaching for her. "Finally," he said.

"Impatience is not a virtue," she said.

"Patience is a curse when it comes to having to wait to hold you in my arms."

"Easily cured," she said, stepping into his broad embrace.

When he ran his hands down her arms, he felt the sheaf of papers she carried. "What's this?"

"The project I did for you."

"For me? I thought—"

"It's for you. And for you to decide what you want to do with it."

Mack took the pages from her hands, waved her into his quarters, and offered her a glass of wine. She shook her head and sat down on the sofa.

He started reading and after a few lines raised his head to give her an inscrutable look.

It took him just twenty minutes to read the pages through and every rustle of paper seemed a death knell in Corrie's heart. She couldn't read his expression and found herself wishing she hadn't tackled the project. What if she'd been wrong? Would she have been wiser to have left the past alone, however badly that past affected them both?

He set the pages down and ran a hand over his face. Without turning to look at her, he said in a choked voice, "Thank you, Corrie. I didn't know."

"You didn't know how much these people loved you?"

"That. And you. I didn't dare let myself believe that anyone could love me this much."

"I do, you know," she said. Her words sounded like the vow she meant them to be.

He turned then, his eyes luminous with scarcely checked tears. But he smiled that sunshine-bright smile of his. "I do know. And I want you to know something, too."

"What's that?"

"That before we checked you out of that hospital, your doctor said you're all better now."

"And that means what, Mack Dorsey?" She smiled and reveled in the shaft of hunger that shot through her.

"That means I'm going to spend the next twelve hours showing you just how much I love you in return."

"And exactly how are you going to do that?"

"I'm a man of action," he said, drawing her up from the sofa and pulling her into his arms. "You said so yourself."

"I'm liking this a lot," she murmured.

He chuckled. "You don't know the half of it."

"Show me," she said.

And he did.

Very, very well.

* * * * *

If you enjoyed what you just read,
then we've got an offer you can't resist!

Take 2 bestselling love stories FREE!
Plus get a FREE surprise gift!

Clip this page and mail it to Silhouette Reader Service™

IN U.S.A.
3010 Walden Ave.
P.O. Box 1867
Buffalo, N.Y. 14240-1867

IN CANADA
P.O. Box 609
Fort Erie, Ontario
L2A 5X3

YES! Please send me 2 free Silhouette Intimate Moments® novels and my free surprise gift. After receiving them, if I don't wish to receive anymore, I can return the shipping statement marked cancel. If I don't cancel, I will receive 6 brand-new novels every month, before they're available in stores! In the U.S.A., bill me at the bargain price of $3.99 plus 25¢ shipping and handling per book and applicable sales tax, if any*. In Canada, bill me at the bargain price of $4.74 plus 25¢ shipping and handling per book and applicable taxes**. That's the complete price and a savings of at least 10% off the cover prices—what a great deal! I understand that accepting the 2 free books and gift places me under no obligation ever to buy any books. I can always return a shipment and cancel at any time. Even if I never buy another book from Silhouette, the 2 free books and gift are mine to keep forever.

245 SDN DNUV
345 SDN DNUW

Name	(PLEASE PRINT)	
Address	Apt.#	
City	State/Prov.	Zip/Postal Code

* Terms and prices subject to change without notice. Sales tax applicable in N.Y.
** Canadian residents will be charged applicable provincial taxes and GST.
  All orders subject to approval. Offer limited to one per household and not valid to
  current Silhouette Intimate Moments® subscribers.
  ® are registered trademarks of Harlequin Books S.A., used under license.

INMOM02   ©1998 Harlequin Enterprises Limited

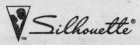
#1225 TO LOVE A THIEF—Merline Lovelace
Code Name: Danger
Before millionaire Nick Jensen headed the top-secret OMEGA Agency, he'd led a secret life on the French Riviera, something agent Mackenzie Blair found hard to believe—until hitmen targeted them. As they searched for the gunmen, their professional relationship turned personal. But would passion prevail, or would death come under the Riviera sun?

#1226 PRIVATE MANEUVERS—Catherine Mann
Wingmen Warriors
When U.S. Air Force Lieutenant Darcy Renshaw was assigned to fly Max Keagan to the South Pacific, she didn't know he was more than just a sexy scientist. He was actually an undercover CIA officer hunting his ex-partner's—and ex-lover's—killer. Intense island nights fostered feelings Max wasn't ready to revisit, but when the killer kidnapped Darcy, Max knew what he had to do….

#1227 LAST MAN STANDING—Wendy Rosnau
A lifetime of lies ended when Elena Tandi discovered her true identity: daughter of a dying Mafia boss. But after years of protecting her innocence, the last thing Lucky Massado, her father's associate, wanted was to entangle Elena in their deadly world. For her safety, he knew he should get her out of Chicago, but how could he walk away from the only woman he'd ever loved?

#1228 IN TOO DEEP—Sharon Mignerey
After testifying in a high-profile murder case, Lily Jensen Reditch moved to Alaska and met Quinn Morrison, her new employer. They shared a whirlwind romance, and she finally felt loved, safe—but not for long. The man Lily helped imprison had put a price on her head, and someone had come to collect—someone Lily would never suspect….

#1229 IN THE ARMS OF A STRANGER—Kristin Robinette
Police chief Luke Sutherlin, Jr., knew better than to fall for a prime suspect, but when she was as sexy as Dana Langston, that was no easy task. The loving way she held the unknown baby in her arms made it hard for him to believe *she* could have murdered the child's mother. However, Luke knew that he had to uncover the truth—before he lost his heart forever.

#1230 THE LAW AND LADY JUSTICE—Ana Leigh
Why were defendants from Judge Jessica Kirkland's courtroom turning up dead? Detective Doug McGuire was determined to find out. Sparks flew as the rule-breaking cop and the by-the-book judge hunted for an obsessed serial killer. But soon the *hunters* became the *hunted*, and if Doug didn't reach Jessica in time, the verdict would be death.